AF265594

CITY
APPOINTED

CITY APPOINTED

WINNING A CITY FOR GOD

a novel by

MICHAEL BURROWS

*A CHRISTIAN FANTASY/REALITY NOVEL PRESENTING
PROPHETIC INSIGHT INTO SAVING A CITY*

 MIKE BURROWS GRAPHICS

© 2017 Michael Burrows
All rights reserved. This book or any portion thereof may not be reproduced or used in any manner whatsoever without the express written permission of the author except for the use of brief quotations in a book review or journal.

First Printing: November 2017, Reprinted October 2022

ISBN 978-0-473-38646-7 (Paperback)
ISBN 978-0-473-65750-5 (Epub)

www.afreshstartbook.com
info@afreshstartbook.com

*This book is dedicated to
my beautiful family and to all those who
love and seek the will of the Lord Jesus Christ,
who know that there is much more to life
than what can be seen with
the natural eye.*

CONTENTS

1

FOUNDATIONS

Liberty skidded down another storm water drain and landed with a splash beneath the city. She looked down at the ankle-deep water covering the stone surface on which she was standing. Eerie lighting danced on the ripples created by the displacement of the waters.

The teenager checked herself over. Her boots were keeping her feet dry enough. The light-weight armour she was wearing seemed to be unscathed by the slide. The locator strapped to her arm looked to be still operational. She could move on.

'They depend on me. I have to fulfil my mission,' she thought. But then another thought entered her mind, 'I wonder how far away it is?' The unknown made her feel a little nervous.

Out of instinct, she lifted her thoughts towards God, 'I know you will help me. You are right here with me and have given me the ability to complete this mission. You have equipped me with all that I need.' As she chose to trust, her confidence rose.

A golden eerie glow in the distance illuminated her surroundings. She found herself standing within the spiritual structure of the foundations of the city. The expanse was like a giant cathedral with pillars towering high above her. The huge pillars holding up the city were equally spaced, each bearing an equivalent weight of the infrastructure above. The rows of pillars seemed to have no end. They looked old, worn by time, but held an ancient beauty, crafted by some primordial wisdom and skill. The supporting structures prevented her from being able to see clearly to the ends of the expanse. Her field of vision was filled with the same sand-coloured architecture everywhere she looked. Nothing stood out to help indicate the direction that she should take. Golden waves of light glided over the stonework. The dancing lines created by the light reflecting off the surface of the water made it difficult to perceive distance.

Focusing on the dark shadows that cut across the waters formed by the pillars helped to anchor her vision. The shadows maintained their depth and weren't confused by the drifting reflections. These same shadows would help to conceal her presence as she travelled under the city.

Liberty hesitated for a moment longer to admire the pillars that branched off at the top, creating interlocking patterns on the roof. "This looks amazing!" she said under her breath as she brushed the hair back from her face. She had never seen this kind of elaborate craftsmanship on such a huge scale before. 'Strange to have such beautiful design work underneath a city where few people will ever see it.' She took a deep breath and exhaled. Droplets of perspiration were appearing on her forehead. It was warm under her armour. She took a step.

Suddenly she heard loose rocks falling to her right and a scurrying of claws. Liberty lunged to the left and rolled onto the stonework that lay above the waterline, barely escaping her attacker's sword as it slashed downwards, striking the platform and producing a mass of sparks. It was a near miss that almost resulted in a slice to her leg. She drew her sword, with no time to think as the demon blade swung through the air again in a wild attempt at her throat. She stumbled backward and hit the wall behind her hard. Her sword clattered against the stones just out of reach, as she slumped to the ground. The demon sprung forward seizing the moment. It stood above her with a look of evil victory. The scaly blue creature was a construction of bones and spines that looked as hard as steel. It seemed to be partially exoskeletal with armour-like plates growing over its shoulders and thighs. Spiny ridges crisscrossed its torso like metal strapping holding it together. Liberty looked up, knowing that there was nothing she could do to escape the demon blade as it was raised high, poised for the deathly blow. Its tiny green piercing eyes exuded evil intent but also displayed a sense of fear and unbelief as if dubious that it was actually in a position to have victory over this Christian girl.

She locked her gaze on the demon eyes, strangely feeling no fear. Even though the beast stood in a place of imminent victory, its menacing eyes seemed to betray it to defeat, unable to accept that it could have triumphed. Feeling fearless, but also helpless, the teenager whispered a prayer, 'God you must help me now!'

At that moment, time stopped, the scene froze. The demon stood, locked in a timeless state. The girl also froze in timelessness.

***

In other parts of the city, the other two teams were unaware of their friend's impending fate, immersed in their own personal missions set before them. They could offer no support. The angel that had been trailing the girl from the beginning, also frozen in time, looked on with grave concern.

***

A prompting echoed through the heavens. It was picked up on the surface. Charlotte Parkinson, who had been getting ready for bed felt the prompting to pray for her daughter. As her knees hit the carpet, a rumbling went out in the spirit. Demons within the vicinity spun their heads around to look towards the source, saw the light, and scuttled away to take cover.

"Lord Jesus..." Charlotte began to pray. "In Your Word, it says... And this is the confidence that we have toward him, that if we ask anything according to his will, he hears us..."

Though unseen with the natural eye, the fabric of the spirit realm was wrenched in to motion as the vaults of heaven opened above her like massive windows in the sky. Clouds, sky, and stars were drawn together into bars and shafts that slide into a gleaming formation. Beams larger than buildings, streets and cities glided through the expanse locking into place. Around the central window, enormous piston-like cylinders propelled through the sky. Massive mechanical-like cogs spun and transformed the atmosphere above into a mass of moving mechanics above her. The central window grew wider than the surrounding ones. The sound of thunder and of clamps securing vaults echoed through the heavens. Brilliant light blazed through the heavenly openings and focused their rays onto the house of the one who was calling on heaven's power.

The fabric of the spirit realm above the house now looked like a massive planet destroyer about to fire on the earth. It was like a city floating in space, upside-down, taller towards the centre. Flashes of lightning could be seen within it as it overshadowed the city. As the light intensified, Charlotte stretched out her arms in front of her. As she did so, a stream of blazing golden light cascaded down on top of her, emanating from the central window of the expanse above. The energy was channelled through Charlotte and shot out in front of her with a flash. Angels and demons all over the city felt the release of power. Buildings shook as demons vaporised in its wake. The temperature of the entire region rose by a few degrees.

***

In a moment of hesitation, the demon who stood above Liberty, glanced over its shoulder helplessly, just catching sight of a wall of raging golden fire. It let out a weak croak before it was engulfed by flames, flinging dismembered body parts far and wide like flaming meteors, only to be burnt up before they hit the ground. The impact happened so fast that the girl was still looking up to where the demon had been as the light passed. The teenager, blinded for a moment, allowed her eyes to grow accustomed to her scorched surroundings. Rumbling trailed off into the distance. Rubble was left smoldering as wisps of smoke rose from fragments of concrete and debris.
Liberty sat for a minute catching her breath, still with her back to the wall. All was silent once again.

"Get up," she told herself. "You have to move."

Back 'on-mission' she pulled her stiff body up to her feet, wiped the dust off her armour with her hands and thought, 'Too close - way too close!'

She pulled her hair back into a ponytail, feeling annoyed for almost failing her mission. She also felt the weight of responsibility as she considered that she was a part of a larger team. She was here for God, she was here for her city, and she was here for her team.

'Where did that explosion come from?'

Still silent. She made a fresh commitment to the Lord always to be watchful.

Her mother got up off her knees, unaware of the impact of her prayer and all that had taken place, but she felt a sense of completion and contentment, knowing that what she had done had made a difference.

2

ANGEL-LIGHT

Liberty sat up with a gasp. She was sweating and breathing heavily. 'What was that!' she thought, 'A dream, a vision? Too real.' She shivered, 'Way too real.'

"I need a shower," she said

"What time is it? 6:45am. Okay, good. I'm not late."

"I really need a shower..."

Half an hour later, feeling refreshed, she started to pack her bag for school.

"Mum, where are my shoes?" called Liberty, flinging a t-shirt off her bedroom floor, revealing her younger brother's toy truck. "If he comes in my room again without me knowing he's going to get it!" she exclaimed.

"Where did you see them last?" Charlotte called from the lounge as she was arranging cushions on the couch before leaving for work. This usual response from mum didn't help in actually finding the shoes, but it at least made Charlotte feel like she was being helpful.

"I went for a run in them yesterday," said Liberty in frustration as a t-shirt and a sweater flew in opposite directions across the room. As another shirt flung from her bed, she exposed her new mobile phone that her parents had just bought her for her 16th birthday.

'Yikes, don't want to forget that,' she thought as she slipped it into her back pocket.

"I think I saw them at the back door," Charlotte remembered.

"You know, you should have got them out with the rest of your gear last night. You don't want to be late for school."

"I know, I know. I'll have a look out back."

"Got them. See you tonight. Love you," shouted Liberty relieved as she rushed to the door.

"Don't forget we are going out for dinner tonight so don't be late," replied mum.

"Oh, and I prayed for you last night. Everything Okay?" called Charlotte after her, but Liberty had already burst out of the house and begun her walk to Gallard High School.

Liberty had a spring in her step that morning. She just felt good about life. The smell of the freshly mown lawn of her neighbour filled the air and the early morning breeze rippled through her light blue t-shirt chilling her a little. She wore her usual black three-quarter compression pants, ankle socks, and running shoes because she had sports for the first period that day. The light jacket with the stripes that ran down each arm was neatly rolled up in her bag should she need it.

As Liberty turned on to the footpath, a streak of light flashed past the edge of her gaze. Over the next five minutes, she counted nine flashes of light. They looked like golden ribbons, alive with energy flitting through the sky. Most of the time they were nearby and trailed off in front of her like a sparkler waved in the night sky. Other times she would see a huge arc streak through the clouds like a comet. She had seen these brief glimpses of glory for as long as she could remember. She called it 'Angel-Light.'

Having been a Christian for most of her life and having attended countless church services, Liberty had seen God move in miraculous ways many times over the years. Even though her church was open to the moving of the Holy Spirit, she had never met anyone who saw what she saw. Liberty had told family, friends and church leaders about the trails of light, but it was quite evident that no one else saw it or could even help her by telling her what it was that had held her fascination over the years. So mostly she kept her Angel-Light to herself these days and enjoyed having her unique 'God thing' just between her and God. God had yet to reveal to her that Angel-Light was a fitting description for what she saw.

It was a typical Friday at Gallard High School, and she had got home in time for the family to go out to dinner together.

3

GALLARD

Gallard High School had problems. Many years ago Gallard had been a popular school to attend, and students from around the country applied for entry, especially those interested in art and music. But in recent years it seemed that creativity had been choked out of the students, and they were agitated in their classes, unable to draw on the natural, ever-flowing creative ideas that used to permeate their minds. Interestingly, Liberty found that she hardly ever saw Angel-Light once she was at school.

The familiar tall, lanky frame of Principal Drake who had marched through the corridors of the school for twelve years had recently been replaced by a younger, more energetic Principal Spurges, with new ideas and a determination to turn the school around and raise it again to its former glory. But unfortunately, even though Spurges had much experience, he found himself fighting an uphill battle.

Drake had decided to resign from the school and run for Mayor of the city, with his sights always looking for higher seats of power. The school had been established fifty years earlier on Christian principles, but Drake had slowly removed elements of faith from school life. For some years in a row, the school had annually invited Kenny Dorsa, a brilliant communicator, to speak to the students about achieving their very best in school and life. But Drake had stopped the regular visits under the premise that Kenny had talked a couple of times at the Christian group. He said that it was prejudiced against other religions to have a Christian speak in the assemblies. In truth Kenny made Drake feel uncomfortable and Drake simply just didn't like him, even though Kenny's positive message and uplifting humour had made him smile from time to time. The Christian group had seen up to forty students attend regularly, but over the last few years, the group had dwindled to three, one of whom was Liberty.

Mr. Hoffman, who was a Christian teacher had allowed Liberty, Bethany, and Sarah to meet in his classroom Thursday lunchtimes for their Christian Group meetings. The three met each week for half an hour to pray for their school and city. The environment of that classroom felt like a haven from the spiritual chaos they sensed around their school. As they prayed together, the girls identified everyday issues that reflected the negative spiritual undercurrents that swirled about them. There were regular fights that broke out on the fields at lunchtime and after school. So for three weeks, they prayed specifically that no fights would break out. During those three weeks and for a couple after that, there were no fights on the field. The lack of schoolyard trouble gave the girls confidence that their prayers worked.

Unfortunately, this year alone, there had been three classroom incidents involving three ambulance call-outs and one fire truck. The fire truck call-out was the most spectacular. In one of the science labs, a student had left the gas on by mistake. Due to an exceptionally unruly day by the students, the final checks of the classroom had not been complete. A group of boys who were loitering outside the science lab after school had wandered around to the back of the classroom to smoke their stolen packet of cigarettes. The classroom had vents in the wall as a safety precaution to dispel any excess gas from the classroom. A spark from a lighter ignited the gas, and a destructive fireball lit up the inside of the classroom, scorching the back wall and burning to a crisp the huge poster of The Periodic Table of Elements that had been stuck up there for as long as anyone could remember. The boys outside quickly scattered, scurrying off in all directions to avoid being blamed for the incident. Just what Spurges didn't need, one of his classrooms going up in smoke. It would be in the local papers for sure! By the time the fire truck arrived the flames were out, but the classroom was smoking with scorch marks up the side of the building.

Spurges, even though tolerant of religion, did not believe any of it. The only religion he practiced was the religion of academics, "Succeeding in academics are the building blocks for a bright future," he would say. He had a good track record, raising the standard in previous schools, but he was new to the city of Riverdale, and Gallard had been his toughest assignment yet.

The truth was that Gallard High School was just the tip of the iceberg when it came to the internal pandemonium of the spirit world stifling Riverdale. There was an assignment against this city. Various prophets who lived in the city were aware that this was a pivotal time for Riverdale. Gabriella was one of those prophets. She had spent many restless nights in prayer, gaining victories in some areas, but being all the more aware that more people needed to be praying for breakthrough and revival for Riverdale. Gabriella saw her engagements in prayer like playing a game of chess. She would see the right move to make and then pray a bishop, or a rook, or a knight, or even a pawn into a given situation. The chess piece may have been a person she was praying for, or some piece of legislation or for a general situation to change. Once she had set it up through prayer, she would allow God to make a move, positioning his people throughout society and continuing to establish his kingdom on earth.

The Lord had revealed to her that he was about to release a new strategy to turn the tide of the city. God had a plan, and that plan involved Riverdale influencing the nation for good instead of evil. He had also shown Gabriella that every city has a mission, a reason for being and that he has placed every city by design. God's purposes are woven into the finest detail, each person is a thread, a part of the tapestry of his eternal purposes. She also met weekly with a group of prayer warriors, and they shared insights together and prayed as the Lord led them.

***

Late that evening, Liberty sat in the back of the car gazing out of the window as her dad drove the family home, having eaten out for dinner. As they passed the General Store, she noticed a boy about her age with a guitar strapped to his back, walking along the road.

'Wonder where he's going,' she thought to herself as three strands of Angel-Light weaved past him.

4

The Save

Caden, the boy Liberty had just seen, stepped into the store to get a snack. He was hungry after having had an extra-long band practice that evening. It was late, and Caden hadn't eaten in hours. He grabbed an energy drink, a small pack of chips and a chocolate bar. He went up to the service area and placed ten dollars down on the counter.

"Late one tonight?" said the store owner to Caden as he slid the change back over the counter.

"Yeah," Caden responded as he took his purchase and turned to leave.

"Hey, careful out there," called the owner after Caden as he walked out into the night.

He stepped back out onto the street and breathed in deeply. The cool night air was refreshing and helped him to feel more awake.

The guitar rested snugly against the leather jacket that Caden was wearing. His red and black checked shirt, with top buttons casually open, suited his ripped jeans. The leather boots contributed to the 'casual Rock Star' image that the band had spent time mastering. Too much 'over-the-top Rock Star' would be classed as 'try hard,' so they introduced just enough 'casual' so as not to distance themselves from their small group of followers that was growing every week.

Caden turned and started for home. As he walked past the park, munching on the bar, he saw two figures struggling under a street light. He stopped and stared, his eyebrows lowered and tightened in a worried expression 'What do I do?' God instantly gave him insight into the knife-point mugging that was taking place. Caden quickly jumped the fence and skidded down the grassy slope, maintaining balance, he stayed on his feet. He felt the anointing of God surge through him.

Full of faith, he shouted at the assailant, "Let him go!"

The attacker turned to face Caden as he approached.

"Get lost, or I'll stab ya!" the assailant shouted in response.

"Drop it in Jesus name!" Caden commanded. The attacker's hand involuntarily opened and the knife struck the path with a clatter. The assailant looked at Caden in astonishment, then charged at him. Caden knew what the power of the Holy Spirit felt like, and he felt it now. He also knew that anything was possible for a child of God. Jesus had said that himself. So Caden put the principle to the test.

Caden stretched out his hand toward the man running at him and yelled out, "Go!"

The assailant was forcefully knocked off his feet to the ground. Even though Caden hadn't been in that situation ever before, he felt that he could handle whatever eventuated.

A familiar verse resonated in his mind: '...with God all things are possible.' Matthew 19:26

The assailant got up, looking bewildered. Not sure what to do next, he decided that it was best not to get caught, so he wisely chose to run off.

Caden called out after him, "Don't come back or I'll smash you to the other side of the park!"

Caden did not think God would throw the guy to the other end of the park. He also didn't want to test God and try that little manoeuvre again, but the statement had the desired effect as the attacker ran off into the shadows.

"Phew, thanks," said the figure straightening out the wrinkles in his shirt, "I was nearly a 'goner,' or at least my wallet was. Thanks for the help. Are you a Christian? I got the feeling you might be when you mentioned the name 'Jesus'"

"Sure am. Oh, and I'm Caden," said Caden as he finally relaxed and reached out his hand with a smile.

"Great! I know the Lord too. I'm Jack. Good to meet you," said Jack as he caught his hand in greeting. "So what was that thing you did with your hand? You didn't even touch the guy."

"Not sure, just happened I guess."

"Well, whatever it was, it saved me, and I'm very grateful. You know what? I've been serving the Lord for many years, and I reckon you have some incredible creative faith. I get the feeling that God is going to use you powerfully in some way and that you are going to have a significant impact in this city. Maybe even in the very near future. Just a feeling I have," Jack said with a glint in his eye.

Caden felt a prophetic anointing as Jack spoke. "Thanks for your word... well, I guess I better get back... hey, nice to meet you."

"I'll see you again sometime. Thanks again," said Jack as he turned back into the night.

As they parted, Caden sensed they would meet again. He also had the feeling that the encounter was more about the two of them meeting than it was about him coming to Jack's rescue. As Caden walked, he turned his head to look behind him, in Jack's direction. Jack wasn't there. The path was empty. 'He can't have run off that quickly,' thought Caden as he spun his whole body and glanced around at the trees to see if Jack had wandered off the path to rest against a tree. Caden appeared to be the only one in the park. He didn't feel scared, but it left him wondering where Jack had gone.

"Anyway," said Caden to himself, "I need to get home."

God had been stirring Caden lately towards something significant. He had felt that God was preparing him for a new season of his life. He walked away thanking God, excited about what possibilities lay ahead.

The next morning he went out for his usual morning run. He found it easier to talk to God while he was running. He started to think about what had happened the night before as he ran past a series of cliff faces, famous in the area as a favourite rock climbing spot. Caden glanced up.

5

insight

A silhouette of a muscular teenage boy could be seen crouching over the edge of a rock face. His form cast a shadow onto the grassy landing twenty metres below.

"You've got a crack in the rock above your right hand," suggested Tristan from above.

"Thanks," puffed Shaun who had been on the rock face for eight minutes. With a few more heaves and lunges, Shaun pulled himself up and over the top.

"Great job! Nine minutes twenty," said Tristan.

"Yeah, not bad," said Shaun who rolled over onto his back, breathing hard on the sunny Saturday morning. Shaun had his shirt off exposing his broad freckled shoulders and hot chest. His short ginger hair couldn't conceal the beads of perspiration that had developed all over his head and streaks began to roll off onto the rock on which he was lying. Tristan, who had fine blond hair and blue eyes, wore a tank top, cargo shorts and a new pair of climbing shoes that enabled him to grip small ledges that regular shoes would have rolled off. Both were into sports and enjoyed pushing themselves physically. Shaun had considered joining the army or the police force once he had graduated college, as he also had a sensitivity for social justice. Tristan, on the other hand, preferred to play a sport for recreation, rather than do it as a job. He felt the call to ministry anyway and enjoyed leading the youth group and felt that there was a place for him in the church where he served.

Shaun picked up the conversation they had begun at the base of the face.

"I have heard God speak to me as I have been reading the Bible," Shaun continued. "You know how it goes – as I read, my attention is drawn to a verse somewhere within the chapter of the Bible that I am reading. From that verse, I get a revelation or a thought of how the verse applies to my life right now. I know that the main way God speaks is through the Bible, but I want to be able to hear his voice in my mind. You know, in the moment. I especially want to hear him when I have a decision to make, just knowing what he wants me to do. In those times I just can't hear him speak to me no matter how hard I listen."

He sat up having semi-recovered from his climb, shrugged his shoulders, and continued, "I know that you can hear God speak to you..." Shaun felt a little defeated with the subject of hearing God's voice.

"Oh well, I guess we had better get back."

"Yep, guess so," said Tristan as they picked up their gear and started down the hill on the west side of the rock face.

It seemed to Tristan that he had always been able to hear God's voice. He had grown up being taken to church by his parents. He had never heard God audibly but usually knew when God was prompting him to do something. Tristan was always conscious of not 'over-sharing' the revelations that God had given him because he didn't want to appear to be a 'know-it-all.' In this case, Tristan felt that the answer was quite simple. It all had to do with faith. It's all about what you believe. You either believe that what you hear in your mind could be God, or believe that what you hear in your mind is only ever yourself. If you think that it is only ever your own words, then you rule out all possibility of God ever speaking to you.

The way that Tristan usually operated when it came to hearing God's voice was to ask God a question, then catch the first thought that came into his mind as the answer. He figured that it probably wasn't the best theology, because what if the first thought that came to mind wasn't God? Though, from experience, Tristan found that God usually got in the first say. It was like getting a 'gut-feel' and then after that, the thoughts that followed were usually his own reasoning, trying to rationalise what he was feeling. So Tristan would take the first thought and ask himself if it sounded like the kind of thing that God might say. He would also consider if it lined up with the Bible. If he felt 'yes,' then he would act upon it and the outcome would usually indicate if it was God or not. The process of doing this helped him to recognise the voice of God more readily over time.

Questions seemed to unlock revelation within Tristan, sometimes even before the question formulated, he knew what an appropriate answer would be. It was a kind of spiritual discernment. He described it as looking at a busy, inner-city scene from the vantage-point of a high bridge. As he looked at the multitude of people going about their daily business, a telescope-like lens would pass in front of his vision and bring a person, way off in the distance, into focus. He felt he would know what to say to that person and that it would bring freedom and breakthrough into their life. With his friend Shaun, who felt that he couldn't hear the voice of God, this was now the case. The revelation was available if only Shaun could grasp it and accept it. One thing that had always intrigued Tristan about these visions was the colouring. The sky was always a golden colour, and there was usually a wash of blue in one direction and a wash of red in the other. He had asked God from time to time if these colours had any particular significance to what he was seeing. Or were these colours just light refractions of his spiritual lens? 'All in good time,' he would sense God saying.

Trying to be as encouraging and yet as relaxed as possible, Tristan said, "You know what?"

"What?" said Shaun who had noticed a gentle breeze beginning to cool his face.

"I reckon you can hear God's voice."

"So I've been told," replied Shaun in an unconvinced manner, but with a smile.

"Yes," stated Tristan. "It's not that you can't hear his voice. Rather, out of everything that you do hear and see and think, it is working out what is God and what is not. The problem with hearing God's voice in your mind is that it is such a natural thing to do. It is so natural that you can easily miss his promptings every day. God speaking to you sounds the same as you speaking to you. Often I ask God to speak to me; then I catch the first thought that comes to my mind. Let's try this – what is the first thought that comes to your mind right now?"

"Breakfast!" stated Shaun.

"Oh," said Tristan, realising that this conversation may not have the desired outcome.

"Yep, I made myself a cooked breakfast this morning, and it was good. Just to get me ready for the climb."

Tristan decided to leave it at that, as they wandered back on to Shaun's property.

"Speaking of breakfast," Shaun said, "I should check I turned off the element on the stove.

As they entered the warm kitchen, they both instantly saw that the element was still on and Shaun ran across the kitchen to switch it off.

"Yikes, lucky we didn't arrive back to flames!"
Tristan raised his eyebrows and nodded once in agreement.

'Breakfast' was from you H.S. wasn't it,' thought Tristan. 'Yes' came the response (Tristan called the Holy Spirit 'H.S.' for short).

"Gotta go," said Tristan. "I'll catch you tomorrow."

"Sweet bro, see you then," said Shaun.

Tristan stepped out of the house, got on his bike and rode through town.

A new café had just opened, so Tristan decided to go in that direction to check it out. As he came up the street, he noticed that inside the café was busy, but only two girls were taking advantage of the afternoon sun on the outside tables. 'They've got the right idea,' he thought, as he turned the corner towards home.

6

AT THE TABLE

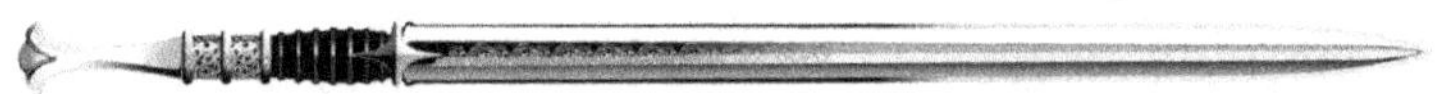

The two stylish girls who sat at the table were Trinity and Samantha who had been best friends throughout their schooling years. Trinity wore a dark grey round-rimmed hat given to her for her sixteenth birthday. It framed her long brunette hair which draped over shoulders. She wore a white t-shirt with the print of the Eiffel Tower, somewhere she had always wanted to visit. Her tight black jeans and black Chuck Taylor shoes finished off the high-contrast black and white look. Samantha, on the other hand, enjoyed injecting splashes of colour into her attire. The bright orange skirt and matching handbag were her 'colour statements' for the day. The denim jacket, white embroidered top, and black boots were appropriate for the trendy new café.

One of the unique things about their relationship is that even though they had been born in different cities, they had also been born on exactly the same day, in fact, just one hour apart. Samantha's family had moved from Bucklands to Riverdale when she was five, because her father got a job opportunity. So Samantha found herself in the same primary school class as Trinity. The two of them hit it off immediately even though they had quite different personalities, and they had been best friends ever since.

Trinity was always up for an adventure and a challenge. Samantha appreciated how Trinity would draw her out of her comfort zone. Samantha on the other hand enjoyed beautiful things, and was an artist. She would encourage Trinity to explore her creative side and also take her to the ballet from time to time, which was out of Trinity's comfort zone.

They felt their friendship was destined by God, not just because they shared the same birthday but because of something else that they had shared over the years. The two of them discovered they would get similar dreams and have similar experiences.

Now that they were sixteen, life was busier. Both were currently studying for exams, playing netball and serving as part of the youth leadership team at church.

Three nights ago, on a Wednesday evening, they had both been sitting together in church and seen heaven open up during a worship service. They saw a waterfall cascading down onto the stage and flowing out over the seats. As they looked intently at the wonder that filled their gaze, they noticed that the 'water' appeared to be a gush of a million diamonds that refracted the stage lighting onto the walls and ceiling. Many people who were standing at the front of the meeting got healed, and about twenty people came up for the salvation altar call at the end. It was an amazing night, but apparently, no one else saw what they saw.

"I feel like something big is about to happen!" said Trinity who sensed an internal excitement, as she sipped her latté. She lifted her eyes to the sun for a moment, causing her to blink a couple of times to clear the moisture that immediately developed around the edges.

The scent of the freshly cut spring flowers sitting in a small vase in the middle of their table, blended with the aroma of fresh coffee grounds pervading the air from the coffee machine busily at work inside the café. Sparrows could be heard chirping from the trees planted along the landscaped footpath. Riverdale was an excellent example of a city that merged parks and high-rises into a busy metropolis that also had quiet, secluded spots where people took advantage to have picnics and engage in a variety of pastimes.

"As I was reading the Bible this morning," Trinity continued, "God highlighted a verse to me from Isaiah:

"By the way that he came he will return;

he will not enter this city,"

declares the Lord.

"I will defend this city and save it,

for my sake and the sake of David, my servant!"

"I felt like God was saying that our city is on the edge of a breakthrough, but also in danger and that we should pray." As Trinity spoke, she felt excited at the thought of being involved in God's purposes. She was aware that forming the words and releasing them audibly made her accountable to her words, but she tended to speak before she thought anyway, so nothing new there.

"I felt Him say that if the two of us would lift up our city in prayer, that He would bring change and that He would bring victory. I also felt an urgency, that the timing of the Lord is close and that we should do it soon. Isn't that exciting?!" She took another sip from her coffee cup and waited for a response.

Samantha smiled, "Want to know what verse God showed me this morning?"

"Absolutely not! … Kidding, yeah of course I do," responded Trinity. Samantha and Trinity shared the same sense of humour.

"Whatever!" responded Samantha, rolling her eyes, then gave Trinity a wink.

Samantha continued, "This is the verse: 'By faith, he made his home in the Promised Land like a stranger in a foreign country; he lived in tents, as did Isaac and Jacob, who were heirs with him of the same promise. For he was looking forward to the city with foundations, whose architect and builder is God.'

"God told me that this is his city. He also told me that he has called a person to come and speak to our city and that timing had something to do with it too."

"Not surprising," Trinity laughed. "I heard that you've got skills. You know, that direct line to God that you have going on."
Samantha smiled and nudged her friend, "Well I heard that you have a red phone in a secret compartment under your bed, and when God has got something important to say, that he calls you first!"

"Yeah, that's right," Trinity joked, "and when I talked to him this morning on that 'red phone,' he said that he was thinking of asking you to be his Personal Assistant. He wanted me to ask if you would mind going up to heaven a couple of times a week to get the latest news to bring back!"

"Okay, I'll go as long as you come with me and show me the way," Samantha replied.

"I would like to, but only the most gifted ones are allowed into the throne room," said Trinity.

Samantha smiled, then they both burst out laughing together.

"You know what though," said Samantha, drawing the conversation back in again, "I heard that an international guest evangelist is coming to town next week from overseas. I think that God wants us to pray for him."

Trinity recognised that 'look' of discernment in her friends eyes as they narrowed, and knew that Samantha had heard from the Lord. She was so grateful for their friendship.

The two of them continued to talk and laugh together. By now, after all this time, Trinity and Samantha were not surprised at how often God spoke to both of them in specific detail about people and events and what he was going to do. God had called them to pray together on a regular basis and more often than not, they ended up praying for Riverdale, praying that God would accomplish his purposes in their city.

Just then a professional looking girl came out of the cafe looking a bit confused and lost.

"Hey, are you all good, can I help you?" called out Trinity in a cheerful voice.

"Oh, I'm just new to town, and I need to get to Fairway Street," said the girl.

"Well, that's not far away, we can take you there if you want. We are going that way in a few minutes," responded Trinity.

"That would be great, thanks so much." she said relieved. "I'm Layla, by the way."

Layla had just stepped off a link-bus from the airport and went straight in to the nearest coffee shop to wrap her hands around a flat-white and to get some directions. The city was new to her, but she liked it already because it reminded her of where she had grown up when her sisters were all still at home. Her oldest sister took up an acting opportunity overseas while her two younger sisters acquired scholarships to study in different parts of the country. Layla, still young in her Event Management career, found great satisfaction in running large events because it suited her 'maximiser' personality and she enjoyed leading a team.

'These seem like friendly girls,' Layla thought.

"Hey Layla, I'm Trinity, and this is Samantha."

"Hi," said Samantha. "Pull up a chair, if you would like."

The girls talked for a few minutes as they finished their coffees and gathered their bags to leave. As they got up, Trinity noticed a 'Specials Board' advertising an iced coffee with a shot of caramel.

"I'm getting that next time!" she stated.

"Mmmm, looks good!" said Samantha.

Trinity also noticed a service area beside the cafe that seemed to lead under the street. 'Strange that it's not locked,' she thought. She saw the padlock lying on the ground.

"Hey Sam, do you think we should close that service area with the padlock? Looks like it's fallen off or something," said Trinity.

"Nah, just leave it. Someone might be down there. You don't want to lock the servicemen in," said Samantha.

"Yeah, I guess so, best not to interfere," responded Trinity.

As they walked past the service area, Layla accidentally kicked the padlock that was lying on the ground as she walked. It scooted along the footpath and slid under the bushes. Hearing the noise it made, but thinking she had kicked a stone or some trash, Layla continued chatting to the other two girls.

As they were walking away, a serviceman came out of the entrance and went to close the door to lock up. He scratched his head and scanned the ground for the padlock. He stood there for a few seconds, shrugged his shoulders and walked off towards his van, leaving the door closed but unlocked.

The girls walked together for a couple of blocks and turned into Fairway Street.

"This must be my stop," said Layla, "thanks so much."

They were outside one of the largest churches in the city.

"Are you going in here?" Samantha asked, pointing toward the double glass doors.

"Yeah, I'm just meeting one of the leaders," said Layla.

"We are Christians too! Is this your church?" asked Samantha.

"No, but I've been asked to help project manage a big revival meeting that is happening next week at the stadium. If you guys are free, you should come," Layla said.

"Sounds great!" said Trinity. "We were just talking about it. We'd love to come."

"Excellent! Starts Monday and goes through every night next week. I'll get you some front row seats, and we can sit together if you want," said Layla.

"It's a date! See you Monday night!" Trinity replied, as Layla walked into the building.

"There is something cool about that girl," said Trinity.

Samantha agreed, "I feel a real connection with her. It must be the Holy Spirit. I'm glad we are going to be catching up with her next week."

7

vision

That evening, the skies were still mostly clear apart from a few clouds that had started to gather on the horizon. The night was warm and still. Lights were being flicked on in houses about the city as people went from room to room, settling in for the evening. Other lights flicked off as people left their homes for a 'night on the town.'

9pm. All was quiet on the street. 'I guess everybody must be in town tonight,' thought Liberty. She was often out with her friends on a night like tonight catching a movie or hanging out at a café or the mall, but this night she felt compelled to stay in and spend some time with God. She made herself a cup of tea and composed herself to pray.

9pm. Caden knelt down to pray in his bedroom as he often did.

9pm. Tristan lay down in the hammock hung by the pool on the back deck of his house, to gaze up at the stars and listen to music for a while.

9pm. Trinity and Samantha began to pray together in Trinity's lounge room.

9pm. Layla sat on her couch and picked up the Bible to catch up on her daily devotional series that she was currently reading.

9pm. Jack sat at a lookout gazing out over the city lights. He could see the airport runway lit up. His thoughts directed heavenward.

In various locations around the city, each of the seven entered into the spirit. Each was unaware of what was about to take place to them and for their city.

Liberty began, "Lord, I lift this night up to you..." The presence of the Lord filled the room, and a vision began to unfold in her mind. With her eyes closed, she saw golden clouds billowing into the lounge from where the walls met the ceiling. It was like the clouds had been blown in from some far off distant place beyond earth's borders, and into her world, her time, and her habitation. Angel-Light circled the whole room, ducking and diving amongst the swirling cloud formations. As she breathed in, her lungs filled with glory, and she sensed the overwhelming love of God towards her. She also felt the joy of the Lord and began to giggle.

"Thank you, Lord, for being here with me tonight."

She didn't want to open her eyes for fear of losing sight of the misty gold surroundings that tumbled about her. But she felt such a strong urge to open her eyes. As she did, she found that she was still able to see in the spirit, that her surroundings were still of cloud and glory. Then something even more amazing happened – the walls of her house fell away. Without the confinement of the room, the glory clouds spilled out over the ground and dispersed as they rolled away from her. Not only was there no longer any room, but there was also no longer any house either. Nor were there any other obstacles obstructing her view from being able to see the entire city. It was like she had been elevated to the vantage point of a high lookout and had an open vista in every direction. She saw her city through the lens of the spirit.

Natural colourings faded and soft orange and yellow hues washed over the buildings, the streets and the parks. The city looked like what you might expect on the night of a bright giant red supermoon. Deep shadows crisscrossed with eerie light highlighting roofs, bridges, and the high points of buildings.

She fixed her gaze upon the several bright spots in the city that blazed with blue-white light. These five primary light sources were distributed evenly across the landscape. The blaze points were bright at the base and extended straight up into the sky like brilliant pillars that reached to the heavens. The light that rose from the bases tapered off at the top, reaching high beyond the clouds to many points like majestic castles with pointed spires. White snowflake-like shapes rose from the base of each blaze point like sparks flying upward from within a fire. The blaze points were buildings. Liberty knew her city and realised that these were churches. As she became more aware of her surroundings, she noticed similar, smaller bright spots, some moving and others stationary. Perhaps these were houses, outreach venues and Spirit-filled people going about their business. She also noticed that she seemed to be standing in the path of a faint blue strip of light running from the North to the South of the city, where her house used to be. The strip of light continued as far as she could see off to the North. As her eyes continued to absorb more detail, she also noticed a faint red beam of light running from East to West, thus dividing the city into quarters.

As the seven looked out from their various vantage points, they became familiar with the spiritual landscape of their city.

Even though the humans were currently unaware of the others that had also entered into the realm, their arrival was immediately felt by other creatures in the realm. Heads turned. Something had changed.

"No!" spat a demon. "He has allowed some of them in!"

An angel stopped in his tracks. "It is time," he said under his breath.

8

MESSENGER

Liberty stood speechless. Her mind was working hard.

'What!?' Liberty thought. 'Am I... is this...? Where am I?'

Then all of a sudden, her familiar Angel-Light shot out from behind. The strands of light wrapped themselves into a form in front of her. The light intensified and spun faster until the individual strands could no longer be distinguished and a flash filled her eyes.

An angel stood before Liberty.

The brilliance lifted, first revealing his boots scorched at the edges. These boots had been planted on the surface of fiery stars, as he had witnessed constellations form around him by the hand of the Creator. The brilliance continued to lift. She could see the richly ornamented hem of his robe. It was drawn diagonally across his body from left to right. The fabric of the hem was woven from the strands of stars and the threads of the origin of galaxies. Half way up his thigh, the hem was worn. The scuff marks and loose fiery strands were the evidence of epic battles and far off conquests. His days had skimmed the surface of some millennia but had been deeply anchored within others, holding his ground until the will of God was dispatched and rolled out over that time and place.

He was a deliverer. A deliverer of messages, a deliverer of victories, a deliverer of revelation.

He stood like an ancient pillar, draped in a robe which cradled fragments of eternity within its folds. The shadows of the folds reached far back through time and space. The highlights of the ridges sparkled with life from another place. If one looked deeply enough into the robe, beyond the outer beauty, one would be able to reach into the depths of the mysteries of God revealed in just one detail of his garment. An expression of the expansive awesomeness of God revealed by a pocket of creation. Every detail, a wealth of revelation of Jesus himself.

His face was carved from the experiences of a thousand lifetimes as he had passed through ages and had remained faithful.

His long hair, splashed across his forehead, had been blown by the icy storms of angelic battle and also whisked by the breezes of the upper vaults of heaven.

The angel's purpose was layered, perhaps eternal. His name was unique, summoned and commissioned from within the council of the holy.

Compared to God this being, as majestic as he was, was just as a grain of dust floating within the vastness of a spinning galaxy.

Even as he looked at her, his thoughts were in other places, on other worlds, across time and other trans-dimensional planes.

"Do not be afraid," he said in a deep voice that echoed around her ears. His words seemed formed from an ancient language that she would not have been able to understand had she not been personally invited into this vision.

"You have been chosen," said the angel.

"I have? For what?" whispered Liberty, trying to maintain a clear stream of consciousness. Her throat was dry; she felt the hairs on her arms rise and her limbs offered no movement. With feet frozen in place, Liberty flicked her eyes left and right keeping her head fixed towards the angel. She felt trapped within her body. The angel reached out his hand and placed it on her shoulder to steady her. Peace drifted through her like an early morning mist settling on a grassy meadow.

"My name is beyond understanding, but you can call me Falcon. I am here to brief you."

She felt renewed strength, and the angel stepped backward. Liberty's body loosened, and she felt the ability of movement flow into it again.

"A personal awakening has bloomed within you because your city has been aroused from its ancient dormancy. God has chosen you and called you here to bring change. God has been preparing you in advance. Your dreams have given you a future glimpse of your quest. There are others like you who have entered this vision, this reality. Together you will draw your city into alignment and save it from an attack that could plunge it into the deepest darkness."

Falcon had a knowing look in his eyes. He waited to see that Liberty understood what he had said and could comprehend, at least a little of where she was. Studying her face and concluding that the message was received, he nodded his head and allowed a brief smile. The angel then lifted his eyes to gaze across the city. Something off in the distance seemed to arrest his attention.

As Falcon turned, Liberty gasped as she saw his magnificent huge wings extending from the folds of his heavy grey robe. The long, silky feathers held an iridescent shine. As his wings quivered with life, traces of blue-green light slipped down the feathers. Two swords, each with a richly ornamented hilt, crossed his back, fitted with belts. As the angel moved away from her, his robe splayed out. She caught sight of armour in exposed places, but otherwise concealed by his robes. The angel advanced a couple of steps, then leaped into the air with tremendous force leaving Liberty a little shaken for a moment.

"Now what do I do?" muttered Liberty to herself under her breath. She started to pace a little and looked down to the ground in thought, feeling alone and a long way from the comforts of her home that had broken apart and disappeared to who knows where. She then lifted her head heavenward directing her thoughts toward God, 'This is just like you Holy Spirit! Falcon could have told me what to do next, but instead, I'm left to work out what to do all by myself. I know you are with me to help, but ever since forever it has been prophetic writings, parables, and promptings. Never a "Hello, and this is your agenda for today Liberty Elizabeth Rose Parkinson!" Why not some direction that is straight forward and easy?' She pondered these things, then as if by a reaction she immediately corrected her theology, already knowing how God worked. She had known all along of course. 'I guess life is faith, and faith is life. I will trust you, Jesus. Show me what to do next.'

"Right, first thing..." she spoke out loud as if to instruct her body to move.

"Find the others... I wonder who they are. I wonder if this is their first time too. Lord, this is so much to take in."

She took the time to drop to one knee in prayer because she felt that it was important to commit herself to the mission that the Lord had set before her. 'Help me to be strong in this place. Use me to complete this mission, show me what to do. Where do I go?' A clear voice sounded from within her, 'You go forward of course.' That was it?! No more instruction than that?!

Liberty took a couple of steps forward. After a dozen paces, the level ground unexpectedly dipped, and her foot dropped down into a depression in the ground. After a moment she realised she had stepped into the impact crater left by Falcon as he had launched. The impression was circular, but it wasn't just a crater, it seemed to have design. There were markings inside it. As she studied the ridges and valleys of the earth, her eyes heightened in their ability to see. It was like she had been instantly endowed with eagle lenses and saw in more detail. The crater was like a richly ornamented compass with a meridian line connecting her position, right where she stood, to another point on the compass on the opposite side. It indicated a direction and guided her line of sight toward a tall building within the central business district. She didn't recognise the building initially but understood that the spiritual landscape of the city would be different from seeing it with natural eyes. The more imposing features of the landscape depicted areas of spiritual significance. Churches were amongst the largest buildings in the city. Spiritual strongholds of the enemy were also significant, revealing where the darkest areas of the city were. She decided that the compass was given to direct the beginning of her journey. It felt right in her spirit, which gave her a sense of relief that she now had a course of action to follow. 'If I'm going to be left signs like this, I'm going to have to be very aware of my surroundings and not miss anything that God wants to show me,' she thought.

Even though she was in an unfamiliar environment, she felt a sense of confidence and also a heightened sense of awareness. It wouldn't take her long before she felt comfortable in this realm. Liberty ran down the hill, skipping from rock to rock. She descended toward mid-city and toward her awaiting mission.

9

ENEMY'S PLANS

Liberty approached what she knew to be Firth Road. She glanced up at the street sign and noticed that the original name had faded and was almost unreadable. Scratched over the top of the sign was a new name, 'Grolg Ravine.'

'Doesn't look like much of a Ravine to me,' thought Liberty, 'Still looks like a road.' She proceeded along the right-hand side of the road following the building line where the shadows were deepest. She became more and wary with each step. She didn't like the thought of falling off the edge of a precipice into some forgotten universe that would keep her suspended in darkness forever. It wasn't long before she discovered the reason for the name change. A few buildings down on the opposite side of the street, she saw three demons carrying an unwilling figure with arms and legs flailing in the air. They threw him off the side of the road, and he disappeared with a cry.

Hesitantly she crept closer. It wasn't that she felt scared, but she wanted to remain hidden from those who were obviously enemies. Her mission lay ahead not behind, so there was nothing for it but to continue in the direction indicated by the compass. She got closer to the creatures. Finding a dark line of shadow to follow, she crept along the pavement until she got to the point where she was across the road from them directly.

From this distance she could quite clearly overhear their boasting, "That's another one fallen for Grolg," said one demon in a raspy voice with a joyous chuckle.

"Yeah, we've done well over the last week. A dozen or so have fallen thanks to us. We may even be in for a promotion soon, eh," as it nudged the first one who spoke.

"Don't celebrate yet, Shroud," said the ugliest of the three. "We have to clear the way before the attack and the final decimation of this city. We still need to rid ourselves of those chosen ones who will bring the most resistance to our advancement. We need to be especially aware of the evangelist who is due to speak next week. There is a lot of activity around him. The church has wised up too and hasn't advertised who he is. With his identity currently kept from us, we will have to move fast once he is revealed. No doubt God will alert His intercessors to hinder our advancement and even prompt them to expel some of us from the realm, so we must not slacken off or get too pleased with ourselves over the few we have already taken out.

"Remember, if you hear of any planned prayer gatherings on the surface, report them at once, so that we can turn away as many as possible from attending. You know what happens once they get started, our plans get dashed, and we have to start again. All a waste of time—a waste of time!" The demon spat on the ground angrily, recalling past experiences and failures.

Liberty couldn't believe what she was hearing, the enemy's plans were discussed so openly in a way that she could understand. Did the intercessors in her church know how directly they impacted the spirit realm? Did they know that they could expel demons and stop their plans? Did they know how powerful it is to gather together? In a moment of revelation, she knew that her personal prayer life would never be the same after overhearing this conversation, brief though it was.

Just then a shadow passed overhead, and a creature landed with a thud a little distance away from the three demons. A small dust cloud rose from its feet.

"Oh great," Shroud growled in a raspy, unhappy voice. "We are being checked on again."

The advancing tall and skinny creature looked a cross between a ragged bat and a cheetah that walked on its hind legs. Folds of skin hung off its bones. It scurried over to them.

"Krow!" the arrival hissed. "How many have you disposed of?!" The bat-like creature obviously had a higher rank than the other three.

"We have disposed of two more today," said Krow. The creature picked up a stone from the ground and scratched two marks into its forearm to keep the tally.

"Good for you. Correction. Lucky for you!" It glared, and then continued, "As you know there has been movement in the realm. A number have just been granted access to enter like an infectious disease."

"Infectious disease?!" whispered Liberty angrily. "I'll give you more than an infectious disease, I'll give you the blade of my sword!" as one surprisingly materialised in her left hand. She calmed herself a little, knowing it was unwise to reveal her position. She also had no idea how she would measure up to facing a demon in battle. As she looked at the foreboding figures, the reality of the situation arrested her again and caused her to crouch deeper into the shadows.

"They are top of our list as the most dangerous now," the creature continued, "I only know the name of one of them, 'Jack' whom I have met in battle on the surface," recalling the incident at the park. "But now that they have granted access they have a better chance at restoring the city. But they must not!" spat the creature. "We have fought hard for the dark tri-references, and while they remain empty shells, without life, we have the upper hand. We won't give them up for anything!" it snapped in an angry, broken voice, but also displaying a hint of hurt emotion.

'Whatever these 'reference' things are, they must be real important,' thought Liberty. 'I wonder if these demons have destroyed them?'

Meanwhile, the demon had composed itself and lifted its head to the sky, and the corners of its mouth turned up in a devilish smile.

'But they are ours!' it confirmed to itself as it spread its wings. Each wing looked like an old sheet stretched across a bony five-fingered frame. The bones splayed out, tapering off to claws on each tip. It flew off into the shadowed sky.

Liberty also looked up to the sky, to where the demon had looked, and noticed the same strip of eerie red light that faintly hung in the air like the nebulaic remains of some distant star that had exploded to its death a millennium ago.

'Is that to what the demon was referring? The red in the sky?' she thought.

"Glad he's gone," said Grolg in a quieter voice, almost to itself. "I always feel uneasy around him."

Liberty was still crouching on the opposite side of the road in the shadows. 'I have to find the others before they get themselves discovered by the enemy' she thought. She was surprised that she wasn't feeling fear, rather more like one who was ready and trained for battle. A verse came to mind, '...physical training is of some value, but the spirit has value for all things holding promise for this life and the one to come.'

'God, you have been training me,' she thought as she remembered the many times she had spent reading the Bible, memorising verses, praying, fasting, and taking steps of faith. She was prepared and ready to serve her Lord Jesus Christ.

She sensed the urgency of her mission and continued along the street, being careful to remain unseen by the demons she had overheard. She darted between shadows and held tightly to the sword. Liberty stopped for a second to admire its warm golden glow. Its surface looked glassy and she could see her reflection in it. Suddenly, to her horror, she saw another reflection glancing off the blade just behind her. A ghastly demon lunged at her from an open doorway bearing sharp teeth, hungry to tear some flesh. She spun around instantly slashing her sword across its form, expertly slicing off its head with one blow. Shocked, she watched the rest of its body slump to the ground. Demon blood dripped down the stairs, but her sword remained clean and glistening. Quickly regaining her composure, she scanned the area to see if the brief confrontation had compromised her position. She set off again, this time at a gentle run. 'I just got attacked by a demon!' she thought, 'I hope I reach the others soon. I wonder if I'll meet this Jack person the demons mentioned.'

10

che gachering

Liberty found the building she had seen from her original vantage point when she had first entered the realm. She quickly stepped around the side of the building, allowing her fingertips to run over the rough brickwork and continued toward the doorway. As she got closer to the entrance, she slowed down and edged forward, not wanting to alert the enemy that might be inside. The opening seemed free from danger, but it was hard to tell if the main foyer was safe for her to enter. She peered around the door frame and scanned the interior. Inside the foyer was an Oakwood counter, some chairs lining the edges of the room set like a reception area, shelving units, a coat stand and some potted trees in the corners to soften the room. Black and white chequered tiling covered the floor space, met by cream coloured walls hung with modern art in appropriate places. On the opposite side of the foyer were some stairs beside an elevator. All was quiet; she waited. 'Better take the stairs,' she thought, not liking the idea of being trapped within the confines of an elevator if another demon was to suddenly appear. Liberty detected no movement, so quickly stepped inside the building, she proceeded toward the stairs. As she climbed the many steps, she felt peace settle over her. There was an anointing in this place. It also wasn't as cold as it was outside. 'This building has protection,' she thought to herself. There was nothing else for it, but to continue up the stairs, right to the roof. She ascended the many flights, filling the air with the echoing tap, tap, tap of her footsteps.

As she arrived at the top and stepped out onto the roof, she felt intimidated by what she saw. It looked like the Council of the Holy. This gathering brought more fear than all the demons she had seen so far. This kind of fear was more like awe, the fear of the Lord. Standing around the perimeter of the roof were five angels facing outwards towards the corners of the city. With flaming crossbows drawn, they stood ready to defend their human assignments. The flames of the crossbows disturbed the veil of darkness like a breeze parting atmospheric curtains, allowing a glimpse into a distant place warmer than here. The fire was restraining the darkness from enveloping the rooftop, so that the council could stand freely, in full view, but undetected. These angels were watchmen.

Standing in the centre of the roof were other beings radiating the presence of God. They seemed different from angels somehow, more human perhaps. The six standing in the centre turned as one towards her. The attention of their eyes overwhelmed her, arresting her senses. Liberty's heart produced a single hard pound in her chest. She couldn't help her mouth from opening allowing her heart beat to be felt in her throat. Her eyes also instinctively grew wider. They wore golden armour. Each person's attire was unique to them, indicating their personality and calling.

All at once she noticed other things that she hadn't noticed until then, such as what she was wearing. She too wore armour. Whether she had always been wearing it or whether it had just adorned her as she stepped out onto the roof she did not know, but she looked like one of them. Her armour had an accent colour of purple, distinguishing her from the others. She also sensed another presence next to her, accompanying her entrance. She glanced up.

"Falcon!" she said. He smiled and then turned to join the other angels in their survey of the city.

'I wonder if he has been with me the whole time,' she thought.

'And on the surface,' came the response in her mind.

'Is he like my guardian angel?' Liberty questioned again.

'Let's just say he knows you,' the voice said.

The response came as a comfort to her. Perhaps he had been with her since her birth or even before.

A member of the council spoke, drawing her attention back to the ones in the centre of the rooftop.

"Welcome Liberty," he said.

'He knows my name?' she thought.

"You complete our number," said the angel.

"Thanks," said Liberty, now relieved to know that she stood among friendly faces. Immediately she recalled the task that had been set for her—'find the others.' Here they are, all together in one place. She knew that they were called by God, as she was, for some great purpose. She could see in their eyes, that even though they were powerful representatives of God, they all shared her questions of 'Why?' and 'How?' and 'What?'

"My name is Jack," said one of the male figures who looked to be the oldest of the group. "Over here we have Tristan, Caden, Samantha,

Layla and Trinity." Tristan waved, Caden nodded, the girls smiled.

"Including myself, there are seven of us," he said.

Caden was next to speak, "I assume that you haven't done anything like this before? This is all way new for us. We are still trying to piece together what we are doing here and what God has called us to do. So far we know that our mission involves our entire city. Like we have to save our city somehow and that our time is short."

Liberty responded, "I can tell you what I learned on my way here, just before I had to chop a demon's head off."

"Wow," interjected Samantha as she shuddered at the thought. "Sounds like your adventure is well under way."

Liberty shared her story thus far about seeing someone being thrown off the edge of the road by three demons. She recounted the conversation that she had overheard as the demons discussed the imminent attack on the city, also the evangelist due next week and the fact that the demons knew that humans had been given access to their realm.

Caden asked, with a somewhat bemused expression, "Where did the guy disappear to? I mean the one the demons caught. Did he like, just disappear?'

"All I know," said Liberty, "is that Firth Road has had its name changed to 'something Ravine', and now it apparently has a massive chasm that we had better not fall in to."

"Yeah, that's right," continued Caden. "So what I'm saying is that we can't trust that we know the layout of our city any more. We have entered the spiritual landscape of Riverdale and there could be all kinds of traps and chasms. So we all need to be super 'on to it'."

Just then a wind blew in from the east that caused all of them to turn towards it. The wind was refreshing, and it felt warm against her skin. Liberty's hair blew back from her face. She breathed in deeply filling her lungs with its energy. The sound of thunder accompanied the wind. As she looked, she noticed a stirring in the clouds that grew as she watched, forming a widening, spinning funnel. A bright light blazed from within it. The light reflected off the armour of those on the building. The concrete surface they were standing on sparkled in the glory. Liberty felt a transfer of energy from whatever it was into her body. She focused her gaze expectantly on the swirling centre. She couldn't help but feel excited by what may appear. The energy that was radiating from the source was captivating. 'Could this be God?' she thought.

With an explosive burst of light, an angel full of brilliant glory shot out of the funnel and soared towards them. The angel looked like a flaming meteorite with ribbons of glory trailing him. He drew near and the glory faded so that they could see him more clearly, or perhaps it was that their eyes adjusted to the brightness. The angel alighted on the roof. He stood twice as tall as the other angels, who themselves were about seven or eight feet tall. The other angels remained steady in their positions, always watchful. The angel that towered above them focused his gaze upon the humans and lowered his six wings. He had four faces, one on each side of his head. You would think that a creature such as this would cause a person to cower in fear, but the effect he had on all of them was one of awe and amazement. The lion's face was the one that looked at them. He also had the face of an ox behind, the face of an eagle on the right and a man's face on the left. He stood, studying them for a time.

"I will feel much more comfortable if he speaks to us from the human face," Tristan whispered.

"Agreed," said Caden, who leaned over, "Do you know who this is? He's one of the four living creatures from Ezekiel's vision in Ezekiel chapter one."

Tristan remembered reading about the creature with the four faces when he was reading through the Old Testament prophets. It was stunning to realise that this angel, recorded in the Bible about 2,500 years ago, was standing before them in reality. It was like seeing a famous person in the flesh. 'It's him, the one from Ezekiel's book!' thought Tristan. After this experience, Tristan knew that his Bible-reading was now forever changed. 'It's all real. So much to re-read, so much more to discover.'

"Peace," was the greeting that the angel offered them. The word sounded like a growl as it was breathed out passing between the lion's teeth. Then in an unnatural movement, his head spun around so that the eagle faced forward to deliver the message of heaven. It took them by surprise and caused Trinity and Samantha to gasp audibly. They all felt vulnerable before him, unsure of what may happen next.

Trinity said afterward that she didn't think it necessary to see a head spin freely like that. "He should have just come as the Eagle in the first place. Like, we had enough to deal with already, without seeing an angel's head tumbling over its shoulders like a dice rolling across a table!"

Liberty's internal dialogue continued to run through her mind, 'Just when you think you have got a handle on the situation, something else completely unexpected happens! Angels, demons, armour, swords, glory, heavenly funnels, more angels, spinning heads. It's all a bit much! Help me to trust you, to lean into you and do what you have called me to do in this place.'

The eyes of the seven fixed on the angel. They each braced themselves for the unexpected.

"Well done to you all having made it this far, but your assignments are only about to begin."

The powerful voice that came from the beak of the eagle was other-worldly. It seemed to have an echo that resounded through their minds. It was like his words originated from another world from within the angel. The words spoken to them, so that they could understand, echoed off into other worlds, unknown by them.

"I have been in the presence of God and have now been sent to you to tell you what must take place. But before I commission each of you I must first show you the beginning, and the commissioning of the church," said the angel.

The angel reached into the sash against his side and drew out a small rod. With one flick of his wrist, each end thrust out to extend to the size of a javelin. The angel spun around and threw it out over the edge of the building. It sailed through the air and pierced the realm, splitting the sky apart, revealing an opening into yet another place. A vision within a vision. The panoramic scene drew back like the opening of theatre curtains for a show, in a semi-circle wrapping around them so that it filled their entire forward field of sight.

The seven gazed into the vision of the past to the origins and birth of the church. As they looked, they understood by revelation, that they were looking back 2,000 years into Bible times. They were looking back through the history of the New Testament of the Bible. As they were taken back in time, from the book of Revelation, back through the Epistles and the Gospels, figures of men and women flashed past. Even though they had never met these people in the flesh, they knew who they were. They saw the apostle John writing the book of Revelation. Next, a raging ocean came into view with a ship sailing on the high seas and smashing into a sand bar. As the ship was being ripped apart by pounding waves and they saw men jumping out into the water. The apostle Paul was helping people off the ship and at last jumped. The waters rolled out of the vision, and a prison cell came into view. Two prisoners sitting in chains were singing praises to God, and an earthquake shook the prison cell. Chains snapped in multiple places, and doors flung open. The shaking crumbled the vision, and behind was a calm sky. A group of men and women were standing on a hilltop looking up at the clouds. Wonder and joy shone from their faces. Then the sky turned dark. It became very dark. A silhouette of three blackened crosses stood, as lightning flickered through the clouds. Truly they were looking at the moment. It was the instance when life and history changed. They felt honoured to witness the ultimate sacrifice made here, and they could feel the weight of all sin that converged in this one place.

Then, in a sweeping upward motion, the entire scene rose high up above them, and they saw what was below. Even darker, even heavier, this was hell.

11

BEGINNINGS

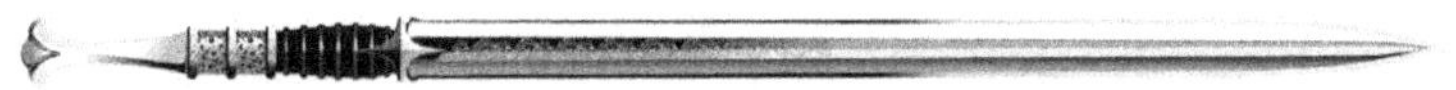

The seven continued to look in to the panoramic vision set before them. They found themselves high above the surface of hell looking down in to it, just moments before Jesus was to die on the cross.

Cold, damp, dark mist swirled and billowed in huge pillars of cloud that extended upward for miles up to the inky blackness above hell. The air was heavy, thick and gloomy. Ominous dark shapes slowly soared on updrafts that periodically sent plumes of misty cloud into the upper reaches of the stratosphere. From that altitude, the high cloud concealed the view of the land below.

A large shadow aimlessly circled in a wide arc toward a plume. The beast had lost all sense of time, gliding through a dark unchanging eternity. No desire for escape, no longer aware of anywhere to escape to, and no understanding of what it was anymore.

Startled, it let out a ghostly screech as a burning ball of flame and energy burst through the atmosphere, plummeting towards the land far below. The speed at which the star shot past would have disintegrated the beast altogether had it been any closer. The creature flapped in a frenzy. Shocked and completely without understanding the beast looked down at the phenomenon, tracking it with its eyes. Already a small speck far below, the white hot flaming star continued to hurtle towards the darklands.

Surface-dwellers lifted their heads to watch the dazzling star continue its decent, lighting up layers of cloud and mist as it unstoppably erased from existence everything in its path. The star fell as the devilish world looked on. The star was not a part of the darkened realm through which it was piercing.

Jesus came from heaven and entered earth. He died and then dropped into darkness. Before Jesus descended, in his last moments on the cross, the columns of cloud and smoke rose up from the darklands reaching up high and seeping through into the earth realm, blackening the sky from the sixth hour.

Jesus finally cried out aloud, "It is finished," and with that, he breathed his last and fell from the cross and through and into the cloudy dark expanse below. This star continued to hurtle through the blackness with an incalculable mass and velocity.

Massive impact!

A deep thud rumbled through the darklands displacing rock and earth. An array of light pierced the thick cloud cover for a moment. The initial shockwave jolted the entire realm. The arrival was felt even to the outer limits of the domain of darkness where form and structure of the darkscape fade into oblivion. A tidal wave of wind, dust, and debris flattened the immediate vicinity and dislodged outer areas. The rumbling continued to roll like thunder through the ground. As the rumbling faded off, silence again settled over the land.

His presence felt by every creature who dwelt within the domain of darkness. Unbearable life and power and light and energy, once known by those from eternity past, but now long forgotten, distanced by the void of lost knowledge and understanding.

The realm had just changed. The materialisation of the star, hurled into existence, had altered death's domain like the needle of an injection, introducing a life-altering drug into the bloodstream.

From the centre of the large crater, the star quickly translated itself up and out, resting on one of the newly formed rocky hills at the rim. The shape of a man visible from within the midst of the star stopped and remained stationary on a high point of the rim to look out across the land. On closer inspection, one could see that it wasn't a man within a star, but the man was the star. He wore a glorified body. He was the bright morning star.

Jesus stood, deep in the heart of hell. The weight of death and sorrow that covered every being like a blanket was peeled off in the presence of life himself. Far off to his left was the faint glow of the lake of fire. In the centre of his gaze were the mountain, the palace, and the throne. He stood as one who had power and authority. The King was here to take what was his and then leave. No need to stay long.

Jesus stepped. Every step transported him closer to his destination, covering vast tracts of ground. Time and space ignored by one who came from a higher place. 'Distance' was merely a sheet stretched out before him, able to be snatched up and tossed aside, enabling him to arrive at any point in the realm in an instant.

A large ancient stone archway loomed high in front of him as he neared the palace of darkness. It was tightly locked up by giant double doors made of carved slabs of rock, far heavier than any earth machine could lift and set in place. Without slowing down, Jesus passed through the doors and directly up to the throne of Satan. Stopping inches away, Jesus glared at Satan with burning eyes. Both closer to each other than they had been since the beginning of earth time.

Every window and crack of the fortress emanated light from the Son of Light inside. Beams of glory escaped through the gaps in the masonry like sharp spears protruding from a carcass. In prideful disbelief, Satan cowered before the brightness that was shining full into his face. Even with Jesus right in front of him, he still could not believe that his greatest moment of victory became vanquished by the resurrection power of the Son of God. Satan continued to stare, as his skin began to smoulder, defiant till the end. He couldn't see the features of Jesus' face clearly because the brilliant glory was too bright.

"I'll take the keys of death now," said Jesus in a low steady voice, as he embraced the ancient ring that hung beside Satan's head, secured to the wall. Three keys hung off the ring, 'Death,' 'Hell' and 'Hades.' Jesus reached out his hand to take hold of the keys. Satan's eyes followed, overcome with defeat. Jesus clasped the ring and ripped it from the wall. Bricks fell out and smashed on the floor, leaving a gaping hole in the wall beside the throne. Without even a second glance at Satan, Jesus leaped with a flash of energy and landed far away amongst the souls who were held in Hades waiting to be collected and relocated to heaven. Jesus gathered to himself all who would accompany him to his Father and they ascended together. The others, already lost, were left behind.

The sky lit up with what looked like multiple lightning storms as souls departed Hades with Jesus. Sparks rose up from the land and into the night sky. Higher and higher the souls of people ascended into the upper limits of the dark expanse. Then they all broke through the boundaries of Hades and shot faster and faster through open space. Stars, galaxies, the universe, and out.

As they ascended rapidly through the expanse of that universe and the next, a thin sliver of light could be seen that stretched across space from east to west as far as the eye could see as the horizon of a new dawn opened before them. The first glimpse of the eternal kingdom. Dazzling brilliance, waves of glory, the sweet hum of a peaceful paradise coupled with high notes that resonated from angelic musical voices melted through their souls, causing them to feel young and renewed.

The multitude approached heaven. Everything about their surroundings pulsated with life. The redeemed stopped at the gates of light. Shafts of solid light shot upwards as far as the eye could see. Hundreds of towering beams perpetually rose without end. All had movement and life; nothing was still. Each beam had a distinct note that it emitted. Each sound was complemented by the one next to it. Together they produced a powerful chorus with each note heard distinctly, but at the same time. Two enormous angels stood either side of the gates. Were they statues, or were they real angels assigned to their positions? Either way, they looked as if they could spring to life at any moment. Beside the angels were six lions on either side, twelve in all. They looked royal and majestic. One dared not stand before them uninvited. The scene of the entrance to heaven was awesome.

Jesus stepped through into the realm of heaven and the sea of souls that followed, whom he had saved, poured through after him. They passed through multiple beams of light. The light appeared to sing. Each note was like was like a jet-stream of wind as they passed through. Jesus entered the centre of heaven into the presence of the Father. Every single angel and living creature in heaven poised in anticipation for one of the most important moments in eternity. As he entered an eruption of song, joy, and triumph raised the entire spirit realm. Heaven resounded with voices, the foundations shook, and thunder rumbled through the firmament of the heavens. The Father ran to meet Jesus. Jesus ran towards the Father. Emotion surged through all of heaven as they embraced. Salvation was complete. Indescribable joy saturated every soul until every soul, for a moment, became joy itself.

Jesus and the Father walked back to their thrones. Eruptions of celebration and song continued to burst forth from every part of the realm, even from the outer reaches. The Father came back to his throne, turned and finally sat. Jesus sat at his right hand taking his rightful place. The glory from the throne emanated unimaginable light.

There was more work to be done. Jesus rose from his throne and yet again journeyed back to the surface to see his friends. He revealed himself to Mary at the tomb, he spoke with the two on the road to Emmaus, and he ate fish for breakfast with Peter on the shores of Lake Galilee. Jesus did many other things as well. If every one of them was written down, then even the whole world would not have room for the books that could be written.

After forty days, he again ascended and took his place beside the Father. Jesus surveyed heaven for a moment; then his gaze moved to the concern of his heart. Jesus looked beyond heaven and fixed his gaze intently at the world. Jesus looked at every person in the world at the same time. The Globe that he had created spun before him and the sparks that were souls shone brightly on the surface. Every spark had a face and a history and a future. Every spark unique and individually crafted and each was the desire of the heart of Jesus. He saw all who lived and who would live on the third planet from the sun. Jesus looked intently, through the vision and gazed at the seven who were watching him.

Liberty's heart skipped. The nature of the vision suddenly changed from being a spectator of a movie, to being in the very presence of God. 'Is Jesus looking at me? Does he know me? Does he care for me? Am I seeing this for real?' It was a shock to transition from being an observer, separated from what she was looking at, to being brought close into the intimate personal space of Jesus. He had locked her in his gaze. His eyes were full of love and warmth and comfort. She wanted him.

"I love you, my child," he said.

It was the most impacting moment in Liberty's life.

***

The age of the world had changed. A new age had birthed, the age of the church, the age of the outpouring of the Holy Spirit. Jesus spoke again, "I commission you," he said to all who had been moved by God to bring his kingdom to the earth.

The commissioning had initiated the next phase of salvation; the call had gone out from heaven and heard by all who lived in the land of time. Ordinary people responded, empowered to do extraordinary things. People equipped with the deposit of the Holy Spirit within them began to fulfil The Commissioning, and heroic stories began to be written, each bringing glory to God.

People began to reclaim cities for the glory of God.

12

commissioning

The vision in the sky ended. The frame dissolved into glittery dust that rained down until it was blown away by the wind. Just then lightning struck in the distance.

"The countdown has begun," said the angel. "That strike signals that our time is short. You have been called to fight with us to prepare Riverdale, your city, for an appointment. Right now there is both an attack mounting, and also an opportunity. An opportunity has arrived for many in this city to accept Jesus Christ as their personal Lord and Saviour and find salvation."

"An evangelistic crusade will begin in the evening, three days from now. An evangelist will deliver a message that will bring deliverance. For this message to be powerful and effective, the Triaxial Identifiers of the city must be aligned. Riverdale must be ready, but right now it is not."

The angel paused to walk over to the edge of the roof. He stretched out his arm to indicate to the seven where to look. He began to point out various locations over the landscape. "The Triaxial Identifiers are the three axes from which the city takes its reference. One axis projects from the throne of the city, which is the seat of authority, and runs along the line of the river. The second projects from the Elemental Stone, which controls the atmosphere, and runs perpendicular to the throne-line, thus dividing the city into quarters. The third originates from the altar in the heart of the city where the two other axes intersect. The altar holds the mission of the city. From this altar, the Mission Axis extends straight up into the sky."

As the seven looked, they could see the faint remains of what must have been the axes. A soft blue glow which seemed to rise out of the river ran through the city. Another very faint red wall of light extended in the opposite direction from where the angel had indicated the Elemental Stone to be. 'Where's the third axis?' thought Liberty, 'There's no visible evidence of the axis that should rise from the centre where the other two intersect.'

"We need to win these three back, the throne, atmosphere and the mission of the city. With these three in alignment, the skies become clear, the truth will shine, and people will accept the message. Life and freedom will come to these people. The time is 'now' for this place, and the window will be open only for a short period. After that, grace will subside for a while. But now there is a momentum of grace, and the wave of grace is about to break. If it breaks and the people are not ready, the wave will break upon an empty shoreline and will drain away as if it had never been. Then will be the wait. The next wave could arrive this year, it could arrive next year, or return in ten years, it could even be a whole lifetime before it breaks again. Do not fail this mission because this is your opportunity."

Liberty felt awed and honoured to be in this position. 'This is my opportunity to make a difference and play my part in history.'

The commissioning angel continued, "We are angels and can only fight when Christians supply faith. Without faith, we cannot win against our enemy. The Holy Spirit has selected you faith-filled ones to form a fellowship that will bring freedom by breaking the strategy of darkness that the devil has been planning and building for the last fifty years."

"Satan has chosen to set up his place of power from here, and his demons have nearly prepared the way for him to do so. To win this city, the enemy must have the throne, he must have the atmosphere, and he must have the altar which holds Riverdale's mission to the world. Every city has a throne, an atmosphere and a distinct mission to the world that is unique to that city. With these three under his control, he will mount an attack to plunge Riverdale into darkness, a darkness that could last decades, even centuries. Currently, Riverdale represents a quarter of a million people, each created uniquely, each very dear to the Creator, each that God has given his life for."

There was a lot to take in, but the seven of them were enabled to follow and understand the commissioning. After all, the commissioning was for them.

"Your fellowship will be divided into three, each with one objective."

"Caden, Tristan, and Jack you must reclaim the atmosphere," said the angel as he raised his arm towards the west. "The atmosphere is important because it influences the lifestyle and the decisions of the people. The air that they breathe sways their actions moment by moment. It affects everybody, from those who govern the city, all through society, to the decisions that children make on the playground at school. It is true that Spirit-filled believers create their own atmospheric conditions, but their influence can either be multiplied or hindered by the greater surrounding climate. The atmosphere has set a countdown, and you must complete your mission before time runs out.

"The atmosphere is determined by the 'Elemental Stone' set high up in the mountains to the west of the city. Normally you should be able to see it from here and from almost anywhere in the city, but the cloud cover is currently too thick and dark. The demons are smothering it until they can gain full control of its power and radiate distorted light over the city. Every city has a primary element, like a personality, which transmits from the Elemental Stone. The primary element of your city is 'Creativity.' The enemy seeks to gain control so that the city becomes a place of creative evil. As you know, Riverdale produces much music, various art forms, architecture, infrastructure solutions, business ideas, inventions and the like. You must gain control over the stone so that this city can bring glory to God through creativity. Jack, you will guide Tristan and Caden through the city as you navigate the best route to get to the foot of the mountains. Tristan, you will lead the climb and Caden, when the time comes you will know what to do. Once you have reached the stone, then place your hands on it in agreement and declare truth over it. Setting the Elemental Stone free is your mission."

Next, the angel addressed Layla, Trinity, and Samantha, "The throne is your assignment," he said as he raised his arm to the north. You must find and fight your way to the throne which sits on a bridge above Grace Falls on the north side of the city. Whichever power sits on the throne commands the laws that govern this city. Even though God's people personally live under the laws of grace, love, forgiveness, blessing, prosperity, and favour, if these attributes govern the whole town, Christian and non-Christian alike will live in the environment of blessing. This city will become a source of supply to the entire nation. The enemy plans to cripple this city and then raise up one or two humans whom he can influence to bring about his purposes. It is his intention to bring harm to this nation. His motivation has never changed, it is to steal, kill and destroy. You will have aid on your journey to the throne. Angels will help you. They will place around you momentary cloaks concealing you from the enemy, giving you just enough time to get closer to your goal.

"Already a weak demon sits on the throne reserving it for the higher power that will come to claim it. You must wipe out the presence that currently sits there. You will have weapons. Once you have eradicated the demon on the throne, the glory of God will fall from heaven and take up residence there once again.

"Once the three teams have completed their assignments, the city will be free; darkness will move out and search for a different place to take up residence. Where the darkness goes is not your concern. Your mission is your city."

Liberty looked around as the others considered the gravity of their missions and realised that she was the only one whose name wasn't acknowledged. Tristan and Caden were looking a little unsure. Jack seemed peaceful enough. Trinity and Samantha were looking at each other with raised eyebrows, communicating that, 'Oh, this is big!' They also were both trying to hide a smile because they couldn't help but feel called and equipped for the task. Layla was also looking around to check out the reactions of the members of the group. Her eyes fell on Liberty.

'Well, whose team am I on?' thought Liberty, 'I'm the only one left. Surely I can't be on my own for an assignment, a team of one isn't much of a team!' She looked up at the angel with questioning in her eyes.

13

MISSION OF ONE

Finally, the angel looked at Liberty, "You will be on your own."

"Great," muttered Liberty who didn't want to be left out. The other six heard what she had said. One of Liberty's enduring childhood memories was going to bed by herself. Her younger and older brothers had shared a bedroom, and they would stay up and talk. She would hear them through the walls talking and giggling and arguing. Then mum would tell them to, 'be quiet and go to sleep!' Her mum and dad had decided that boys and girls should be in separate rooms. The only problem with that is that she never had anyone to talk to in bed. But this was when she started to discover that she could speak with the Holy Spirit and he would talk back. Even from the age of six, she knew when the Holy Spirit was communicating with her. Again, she was back to being by herself.

"You are the most equipped of all of us," said Trinity.

"What? Why?" said Liberty surprised by the comment.

"You shine brighter than the rest of us. Didn't you notice?"

"Oh!" Liberty looked at herself, and it did appear that she had extra detailing in her armour and yes, perhaps her glow was slightly stronger than the others.

"I felt intimidated when I saw the rest of you," she said. "I didn't notice too much of what I looked like."

"All I can say," said Samantha, "is that when I saw you, I felt even more confident that we had an awesome team!"

"Thanks," said Liberty, now a little self-conscious, being the centre of attention. But she straightened up and looked at the angel again who had been patiently waiting as she was coming to grips with the fact that she would be working alone.

The angel spoke again, "The best chance you have to gain access behind enemy lines and make it to the altar is alone. Two or three of you will not make it through unnoticed. You must be agile and slip through gaps and openings that we make for you. There will be angels working with you, but you may not see them."

Your first task is to find the 'Mission Keys' of Riverdale. Without those keys, the city will drift from its purpose. The enemy will be able to distort its path and even use its strengths to invite darkness to envelop the land."

Liberty wanted to ask what she should do with the keys once she had them but the angel's gaze had Liberty's eyes locked on his. She couldn't break the gaze even if she wanted to. She stood, almost mesmerised by his appearance and forgot to ask the question.

"This is your task, and you alone must complete it. Once you have the keys, you will know what to do. Do not let them out of your sight. Currently, your city has forgotten its mission to bring glory to God through creative art forms that will influence your nation and other countries of the world. When all of you succeed in your assignments, this mission will be resolved."

The angel then broke off his gaze and surveyed the group. He addressed the entire fellowship, "Each of you must maintain some awareness of the progress of the other two teams so that you can pray and combine faith when required. If you are listening to the Holy Spirit, you will sense his promptings to pray. Make sure you heed these promptings as they could be a matter of success or failure, life or death.

"Be very careful, if you die in this vision, it will end for you and your objective will be lost. All three objectives must be fulfilled to win your city; otherwise, it will be left open for attack. We have only one opportunity available to us, and it may not open again for years, or ever.

"The outcome is not a certainty because it doesn't just depend on you alone. It also depends on those who are prompted to pray for you from the surface. Your mission will not be disclosed to the surface because obedience and faith are required to bring victory. After that, the Holy Spirit will reveal to those who have partnered with us, some of the impacts of their involvement. The Bible says, 'But whenever anyone turns to the Lord, the veil is taken away.' It happens afterward. First a person steps out in faith, and the after that the veil is taken away and the results can be seen."

14

on the move
- mission liberty -

The angel handed Liberty a locator that she secured to her forearm with a strap made of robust leather. A lace criss-crossed the holes that were punched into the edges of the leather so that the ends could be drawn together and tied to the underside of her arm. The exposed side of the strap had a jewel-like dome protruding from it. Through the protective dome, she could see a digital map of the city. The layout, indicating her position, would help direct her to the keys. She was also given a pack to carry the keys once they were in her possession.

Liberty was first to set off.

She ran down the stairs and made her way to the entrance of the building. She stood in the doorway and studied her locator. The device displayed a map lit in green wireframe to indicate roads and buildings. The image dynamically scrolled on the screen as she moved, with her position always marked in the centre of the locator. Beside the screen were a couple of buttons. She pressed one of them, and it gave a zoomed-out view of the city. She noticed an orange glowing point on the screen. She tapped the surface of the dome close to the orange point on the map, and it magnified to its general location. From what she knew of the city, it looked like the keys were around the area of the old library. 'This must be where I'm heading,' she thought. As she tucked the loose strand of hair behind her ear, she pressed the other button on the locator which immediately produced a soft light that radiated from the dome. The light wasn't very intense. 'That's not going to help me much,' she thought.

Liberty headed towards the library, keeping within the shadows cast by the buildings that lined the streets. Only now did she wonder why the city was so sparsely populated. She hardly saw any people or angels or demons. 'Maybe things are being filtered out for me; only seeing that which I need to see,' she reasoned. Liberty decided to quicken her pace. She broke into a jog. Feeling good, she tested her skills. Coming up on her left was the entrance to a large hotel. In front of the double doors was a flight of concrete steps framed between sloped metal rails that ran down each side of the entrance. As she approached the steps, she pushed off the ground with her left foot and landed high up on top of the first rail. In one smooth movement, she pushed off with her right foot and landed in the middle of the staircase. She then ran a couple of steps, jumped up on to the second railing, spun around in a half turn and did a backward flip off the rail, landing gracefully on the other side. She did a half spin to face forward again and saw a row of bushes that lined the sidewalk, she ran and dived over them, combining a twist and a forward flip as she sailed through the air. She landed in a roll and finished in a crouched stance on the other side of the bushes, with her fingertips splayed out on the concrete to steady her landing. Maintaining her crouched position she looked up to assess her surroundings again. Feeling equipped and capable, she allowed a smile to broaden across her lips. Her eyes twinkled, they were windows through which could be seen a glimpse of stars at the outer edges of a galaxy, spinning somewhere deep within her. She set off again.

The hotel stood on the corner of a crossroad. Liberty came to the end of it and turned into Banks Alley. Banks Alley was a short-cut she would often take whenever she was walking from home to the train station. She did this frequently as she would visit her gran and grandpa who lived 20 minutes away by train. It was a convenient shortcut to take because the end of it was only a few minutes from the station. This time she was running down the alleyway for a different reason, not to catch a train, but to save her city. The gravity of her mission sent a shiver through her. She did her best to shake it off the feeling as she neared the end of the alley.

Just before she got to the end of the narrow path between the buildings, about to step out into the open, a large shadow passed overhead. Liberty quickly jumped up a small flight of stairs into a doorway and pressed herself against a wooden door in an attempt to conceal herself from the creature above. The door was hard, and the stonework of the wall next to it was cold. Droplets of sweat started to bead on her forehead. 'Has it seen me?' she thought. She inched her head out into the open to see if it had passed. The skies were clear. She crept towards the end of the alley which opened out on to Princess Street, usually a busy road in the heart of the central business district. She peered around the corner, and her eyes widened as she saw a monstrous dragon a short distance away that had landed in the middle of the street. With its wings splayed out, their span nearly touched the buildings on both sides of the road. The grey lizard-like creature looked fearsome with thick hexagonal scales locked tightly together across its body. A row of raised horns protruded from its back and ran down to the end of its tail. Its wings stretched wide, revealing an underside that exhibited bright orange streaks that traced around the edges of its scales. Its proud face looked ferocious, displaying an evil intelligence that made it look formidable. The dragon's landing caused dust to rise from the streets. The dust was stirred up and swirled around its thick legs and bulging belly. Liberty looked closer and saw that the clouds were falling from the dragon itself. Liberty realised that the dust clouds were not from the street, but that she was looking at the tangible presence of the dragon, rolling like mist off its back. Its presence could be seen and felt. But the aspect of the dragon that sent chills down her spine the most was its eyes. They blazed a fiery, piercing orange. Nothing could escape its gaze.

As she looked, the dragon's head turned and staring straight into her eyes it let out a screech. Suddenly she was drawn into within inches of the dragon's face. She could see nothing but the head of the dragon. Its presence was like heatwaves diffusing the edges of her vision, but directly in front of her, she saw every horrifying detail, magnified and way too close. Its thick bumpy skin shimmered as heat radiated through its scales. She felt caught in its claws. Her forehead went cold and breathing shallowed as she stared full in to its face. Then suddenly she was drawn back to the place where she had been standing at the end of the alley. It was as if she had been given an alternate viewpoint for a moment. The proximity jump, initiated either by the dragon or by an ability of hers that she didn't understand yet, made her heart almost jump out of her chest and physically knocked her to the ground.

She scrambled to get up. Two demons slid off the dragon's back and commenced the pursuit.

She turned and ran as fast as she could back up Banks Alley. With her wits still about her, she turned left taking a different route towards the library. She could hear the screeching echoing through the buildings. She didn't want to look behind, but ran as fast as her legs could carry her. 'Where do I go? Where do I hide? Help me, Jesus.' All she could think was, 'I must get underground; I don't want to see that dragon ever again!' She took a quick glance behind her, and to her horror, more demons had joined in the pursuit. There were five now chasing her, and she could see the head of the dragon rising from beyond the row of buildings. She let out a half scream - half cry, and felt that her legs might buckle under the pressure. She was almost running too fast for her legs to catch up.

With tears streaming from her face she called out desperately, 'Help me, Jesus.'

A soft, warm word came into her mind, 'I'm here.'

'Help me God!' she repeated.

'You can do this,' said the voice.

'Save me!' Liberty pleaded.

'To the café,' the voice responded.

The words came clearly. Liberty obeyed.

15

ASCENT

- mission boys -

Back on the roof, the boys prepared to set off. Two of the angels who had been standing watch at the perimeter of the building broke off from the formation and followed the boys from a distance.

The companions were not complete strangers to each other. Tristan and Caden went to the same church. It was a large church, and the two of them were involved in different leadership teams. Caden had only been at the church for a year but was already a key member of the worship team. Tristan had been attending the church for some years and spent much of his time investing in the youth that he was leading. The two of them had a few conversations and laughs over the year, and were pleased to see each other on the rooftop. Even though Jack and Tristan had met for the first time at the briefing on the roof, Caden and Jack were already acquaintances through the unfolding of the previous night's events in the park.

The boys hurried down over a dozen flights of stairs, eventually reaching ground level. They looked toward their goal and considered their next move. The streets were empty.

"The enemy must be gathered elsewhere. Perhaps getting a briefing before the attack," suggested Caden.

"Could be," said Jack. "Anyway, that's not our concern. Our assignment is to get to that Elemental Stone as soon as we can."

"Have you done this before Jack?" asked Tristan. "I was curious as to why the angel specifically spoke to you about leading us to the foot of the mountains."

"Not quite like this. Let's just say that I have a fair idea where demons could be hiding in the city. You will have to lead with the climbing aspect of the mission though. That's new to me."

"I've climbed some of the faces before, though never to the summit. But that's not going to do us much good if we don't have climbing gear."

"I'm sure the Lord will provide. He wouldn't send us unequipped," Caden responded. Surely such an important detail hadn't been overlooked by the commissioning angel. "Anyway, I'm glad we don't have to lug heavy ropes and clips around the city. Though there better be some climbing gear is waiting for us when we get there or we aren't going to get very far."

The three hurried their way through the city. There wasn't much demon activity around. Their path seemed to be clear. As the three passed by Taylor's Book Store, they were unaware of a presence that had caught sight of them as they hurried down the narrow street towards the mountains.

"Got you!" a demon chuckled to itself. The insect-like demon scuttled into a nearby building to report the sighting. It found a messenger, a large Blackbird with oily feathers, very quick and efficient in its delivery of messages and assignments.

"We have them," Scrathe said to the bird. "Clear the way for the hopefuls. They must be heading toward 'The Darkness.' It will be more efficient and clean to attack while the three are on the cliff face, rather than in the city with options and places to run."

"Understood," said the bird in a high-pitched gravelly voice. "Even if they could make it up to the top to reach The Darkness, there is nothing they can do now. The transformation is almost complete, all that disgusting elemental rubbish will soon be forgotten, and even the angels will call it what we have called it all along."

"It's just a matter of time," said Scrathe. "Once its transformation is complete and the stone turns dark, we will initiate our attack. We have our man. Drake is running for mayor. If we get him in, he will bring order. This strategy is what we have been so painstakingly outworking. Our man Drake will help us to run all the Christians out of town, and the rest who won't leave will convert. Once we have Riverdale, we can set up at least two or three new highways for the Master!"

***

A realm away, back on the surface, Tristan's dad Max was getting ready for bed. He opened his Bible, as was his custom during the evenings. He liked to close out the day by reading something from the Proverbs or the Psalms and then pray for various people as the Holy Spirit directed. He opened the Word and began reading Proverbs 31. Almost immediately verse two caught his attention.

'Listen, my son! Listen, my son, the answer to my prayers!'

Max would pray for his family each night anyway, but at that moment he lifted up a special prayer for his son, as directed by the Holy Spirit. "I pray for Tristan tonight Lord; I pray that you would answer his prayers, provide for his needs and wants. Lead him on your path, to the mountain tops of your presence. In Jesus name, Amen."

***

At the moment he said 'Amen,' three sparks shot out from Max's hands like fireworks, unseen by Max, but visible to the spirit realm. The sparks quickly rose into the sky like flares and arched over the landscape far below and tore through the clouds towards Razor Peak. As the prayer sparks descended towards the boys, two flying demons who were patrolling the skies rushed towards the sparks in an attempt to stop them or at least slow them down. But their deflectors had little impact on the simple, but powerful prayer that Max had prayed. In a blaze of light, the sparks smashed the deflectors from the hands of the demons. Both demons were smacked away in opposite directions and helplessly flung through the air. The trajectory of the prayer did not shift in the slightest due to the fact that Max prayed regularly with faith and confidence. The demons would think twice before attempting to intercept another prayer spark from Max.

As the sparks descended towards the boys, each spark stretched into a beam of liquid light that morphed into specific answers to prayer. The first beam to hit its mark and spiralled around Tristan's arm and waist. The second streaked down over Caden's shoulder and back, and the third splayed out over Jack's back and down his side.

The boys, unaware of the incoming prayer, arrived at the base of the cliffs. Climbing ropes materialised over Tristan's shoulder. A harness appeared around his waist with carabiners and pegs clipped on to it.

"Wow! Nice," said Tristan admiring the newly acquired gear. Then a crossbow materialised over Caden's shoulder along with a quiver full of arrows. Each arrow had a different tip, each for a different purpose. The third spark that had splayed out over Jack's back morphed into a light shield that strapped itself to him, along with a sword secured to his side.

"I guess we are equipped with everything we need," said Caden smiling, feeling much more confident and even looking forward to getting locked into battle, especially with the angels present to cover their backs, though he hadn't seen them for a while now. 'I wonder where those angels have got to that started to follow us,' he thought. He realised that he hadn't seen them since leaving the building. 'I hope they aren't too far away.'

From the base, the cliffs looked dauntingly high. It didn't help being unable to see the top due to heavy cloud cover. Or perhaps it did help being unable to see how far they would have to go. Tristan examined the first rock face.

"It's going to be a long climb," he said, "but not very technical. There seem to be plenty of hand holds, at least as far as I can see."

There were a couple of tricky parts that he would have to work out once he got to them.

"You see those two ledges cut into the cliff, way up there over to the right?" he pointed out. "Well, our best course is to make our way to that first one, and from there head for that one higher up," he said highlighting the ledges that would serve as rest areas for them. Tristan had never climbed to the top of Razor Peak before, not even half way, but he didn't mention that to the others.

He began the free-climb so that he could secure pegs and ropes for Caden and Jack to follow. It was slow going, and Tristan felt less confident now that he clung to the face and falling was a real possibility. He reached his left hand high and felt a decent sized hand-hold. 'Great!' thought Tristan as he pulled himself up inspecting the hold, 'A crack in the rock, perfect for the first anchor.' He hammered in the anchor. Chink, chink, chink went the hammer as he drove the metal peg into the hard stone.

"Okay, it's set for you to follow. I'll continue up to secure the next anchor," called Tristan.

After some minutes, Tristan glanced down, having now secured five anchors. "Are you guys doing Okay?" he called down.

After a pause, "Doing fine," came the response.

"Keep going. We can rest soon."

There were no more responses from Caden who was using all his strength to grasp handhold after handhold. Jack was trailing him and was also conserving energy, focused on the climb.

Quarter of an hour later they were all up breathing hard on the ledge. After a brief rest, the boys continued their next ascent.

Tristan was now about thirty metres from the ground. As he took a break to gaze over the city, he noticed for the first time some dark shapes silhouetted against the grey sky circling some distance away from the cliff face. 'What are those?' he thought to himself, 'Oh no, I think those are the enemy.' He felt his heart sink. 'How long have they been there?' he wondered, 'I hope they haven't seen us. Wishful thinking,' he told himself, 'They would have to be blind not to see us.'

16

SLIDE

- MISSION GIRLS -

The girls were the last to leave the rooftop. They broke away from the fellowship and proceeded north toward Grace Falls.

They walked carefully but quickly along The Parade, one of the main roads leading out of the city. Within the centre strip, separating the inbound and outbound traffic, grew a line of palm trees which cast intricate shadows across the sidewalk helping to conceal the girls. 'But it makes enemies hard to see too,' thought Layla, feeling uncomfortable with the lack of visual clarity ahead.

As they neared the outskirts of the Central Business District, The Parade split off into two highways with 'Fountain Square' between them. The square was surrounded by buildings and had a large stone fountain in the middle of it. The girls opted to take the longer route around the edge of the square, rather than choosing the more obvious but exposed route through the centre of the square. Beyond the square lay the regional park which covered over ten square kilometres and within the park, amongst the trees, protruded Grace Falls.

They got to the tree line with no apparent difficulties. Ahead of them, they had the challenge of picking their way through trees and open country without being seen. No demons had appeared so far, but that didn't mean that there wasn't any there, so the girls remained cautious. Leaving the familiar geometric landscape of the city behind them, the girls began their journey through the wooded wilderness of the regional park. The atmosphere was damp amongst the trees. Dew had settled on the leaves and was beading on their armour. It felt uncomfortably humid inside their clothing, but it was cold enough outside for them to see their own breath as they trudged through the heavy undergrowth. Now and then a tree would creak as if warning them to turn back and the periodic empty rustling of leaves in the breeze made them feel very much alone. 'I don't like this,' thought Samantha, 'I'd rather be back on the rooftop within the safety of those surrounding angels.'

"Down now!" said Layla in a sharp hushed tone, reaching out to her friends to drag them to the ground. They all immediately crouched. "Look, over there," she said pointing towards a ridge in the distance surrounded by tall trees. They could see dark shapes hovering over the ridge. The hooded creatures were a far enough away in the distance for the girls to feel confident that they were still safe. As they looked, the demons seemed to be gliding in circles around each other.

"What are they doing?" asked Trinity.

"I have no idea, but they are spooking me out," said Layla. "Let's keep moving as quickly and quietly as we can."

A sudden chill brushed through the leaves around them. The girls walked on, keeping to the left of a line of bushes which obstructed their enemy from being able to see them. Trinity led the way. The row of bushes ran along the edge of a steep bank that dropped off to their left. Up ahead, the tree line drew closer to the verge, narrowing the area of ground that they could walk along. As Trinity took her next step, the earth under her feet gave way and she started slipping down the bank, taking rocks and loose branches with her, starting a small landslide. Samantha and Layla looked down at their friend as she was sliding away. The sound of falling rocks and snapping branches gave their position away. The figures turned in the direction of the girls, letting out a unified screech. The three dark shapes immediately started gliding towards them with terrifying speed. The figures that were once a long way off in the distance were closing in on them fast. They could never outrun these creatures.

Layla grabbed Samantha's sleeve and pulled her down the bank after Trinity.

"Go now!" said Layla with urgency as they slid. Covered in dirt and soil, the two girls dropped down off the end of the bank onto a clearing beside a stream below. Trinity lay beside them holding her ankle with an expression of pain on her face. Layla and Samantha got up either side of their friend and grabbed a shoulder each. Placing their arms under hers, they pulled her out of sight, to the foot of the bank.

"Trinity, are you okay? The demons are here!" said Layla.

"I don't know," said Trinity with gritted teeth, "I might be able to walk. Where are they?"

"Above us," said Samantha. "We need to get out of here now, they are coming to investigate the slip."

"Can you get up?" asked Layla

"Have to. Get me up and let's go!" said Trinity.

Supported on each side, the girls raised Trinity to her feet. Trinity groaned as she tried to put weight on her foot.

"Come on, move, don't worry about me," said Trinity.

The three friends edged their way along the base of the bank, over the leafy undergrowth.

Layla looked up to where she had been and caught a glimpse of a dark figure descending the bank. "They're coming," she said alarmed, "but they seem to be going straight down the slip instead of tracking across in our direction. I don't think they've seen us yet."

"We'll never outrun them if they do. Quick, over there." The gorge curved around to the right. An overhanging tree with exposed roots created a cave that could serve as a hiding place. Layla and Samantha dragged Trinity into the alcove, and they all pressed themselves together against the bank breathing heavily. They waited for what seemed like endless minutes. They heard nothing and saw nothing. The three girls, breathing hard waited in crouched positions daring not to make a sound. Trinity was clasping her ankle with her eyes scrunched up trying to control the pain.

"What should we do?" whispered Trinity finally.

"One of us could take a look."

Just as Samantha moved to look, she saw a black-cloaked figure shoot off through the bushes in the direction of Grace Falls. Samantha held her breath again and quickly pushed herself back as far as she could into the alcove. Its speed made the girls feel very aware of their own limitations and their lack of ability to escape from the unearthly creature. A second hooded creature rushed off through the trees in a slightly different direction ahead of them. 'What about the third?'

thought Layla. The girls waited. Just then the third dark, ghostly figure blew past them at a slower pace along the edge of the bank. They waited. Layla lifted her thoughts to God, 'Lord protect us.' All was quiet apart from the wind in the leaves.

After some time Samantha spoke, "I don't want to leave the safety of our hiding place, but we are going to have to take the chance so that we can complete our mission."

"What about you Trinity, can you walk?" asked Layla.

"Pray for me. Come on – let's use our faith!" said Trinity, her face still showing signs of discomfort.

"Yeah," said Layla. "Let's do it!"

"I've got this one," said Samantha. She placed her hands on Trinity's foot and prayed, "I declare healing over Trinity's ankle in Jesus name. I pray that you would fix her. Remove all pain and help her to walk again."

Layla also reached out her hand and prayed, "Yes Lord, your Word says that you have taken our sicknesses and infirmities upon yourself and so we claim it healed in Jesus name!"

Trinity got up and tested it.

"It's a bit stiff, but not as painful. I'm going to claim my healing anyway and walk it off. Let's go."

17

GRACE FALLS
- MISSION GIRLS -

Layla, Samantha, and Trinity reached the base of Grace Falls and rested on a rocky outcrop beside the river. It was concealed on three sides by bushes and trees but gave them an excellent view of the falls. Trinity and Samantha who had grown up in the area knew this part of the Park intimately. They had both spent sunny weekends and holidays swimming in the river and had gone to outdoor concerts during the festival months.

Layla had visited the park a couple of times and had walked the path to the top of the falls that took an hour at a comfortable pace. However, she had never seen the falls from the perspective of the spirit and was amazed by what she saw. The spiritual form of the falls was spectacular, as it should be, for it cradled the throne of the city. There were spires and turrets and all kinds of palatial structures that layered up the cliff face either side the falls. The citadel that surrounded the falls was high and lofty. It was unmistakably the place from where the city was ruled.

"Isn't it absolutely beautiful," exclaimed Samantha.

"Wow, the colours are dazzling," said Trinity in wonder, thankful to have something to take her mind off the throbbing of her ankle. "Such a contrast to the darkened landscape that we have been traveling through so far."

"I know. I'm never going to look at these falls the same way again once we are back on the surface," Samantha added. "I only hope that we can secure the throne so that the enemy can't claim this place as theirs. But when we are back, wouldn't it be amazing to be able to see all of this the way we see it now."

"Yes," agreed Layla. "I hope we will be able to see everything in the spirit once we are back. I would hate to return being unable to discern all of this." Then lost in thought, she added, "How amazing are the spiritual influences that constantly ebb and flow around us every day."

Trinity spoke again, "I don't think that God would call us here as a one-off event and then just leave us as we were. Perhaps his plans for us may be even bigger than our current assignment, as necessary as this one may be." The girls nodded in agreement as they continued scanning their surroundings.

The spiritual activity around the falls was much more intense than they had seen anywhere else so far. Both angels and demons were on assignment. Some flying up through the falls and others walking into the palace. Each seemed to be about the business of their individual tasks. Small groups of demons walked together, keeping their distance from the angels who would breeze past. Angels would walk or fly in ones or twos, engaging each other, but practically ignoring the demons.

After some time Samantha said what they had all been thinking, "So, how are we going to get to the throne ladies?!"

"Isn't it obvious?" said Trinity. "I thought you were going to go out there and use your wit and charm on one of those angels, and get him to fly you up."

Samantha looked back at Trinity with eyebrows raised accompanied with a smile, without the need to respond verbally.

Trinity shrugged, "I'm just saying that I'm sure that the angels will help us if we can get their attention. We will need a guide anyway so that we don't waste our time going in the wrong direction. It looks like there is a lot of 'palace' to navigate."

"That's a good point," said Samantha "I think we need some help, even if it is only to create a diversion so that we can get into the palace for a start."

"So the question is," said Layla thoughtfully. "How do we engage an angel? The other question would be, is it possible to engage them from a distance? I don't know much about angels, but I do know that what we believe either permits or hinders God's plans for us. Our belief in what the Bible says activates the spirit realm, and I'm sure that without the faith of people, we limit angels in the ways that they can help us. It is faith that determines the relationship between them and us."

"So anyway, that said," she continued, "I'm going to try something…"

Layla stepped out further onto the rocky outcrop and spotted two angels walking together who were still some distance away from the entrance of the palace. She started to pray. 'Lord, I pray that you would tap those angels on the shoulder and get them to come over here.' As she directed her thoughts towards them, one of the angels looked up and glanced around, drawing the others attention. They both stood still and looked out across the water in a way that someone would look if a stone had been thrown and had struck them on the back. Even though they were some distance from the falls themselves, Layla could see the surprised expression on the angel's faces. As the angels continued to scan the waters, one caught sight of Layla, a lone female figure standing motionless under the trees on the rocky outcrop across the water. Exposed in full sight, she suddenly felt vulnerable and at the mercy of what would happen next. 'Is this a good idea or not?' The angel who had spotted Layla discreetly pointed her out to the other, trying not to draw attention to themselves or alert those around them. The first of the two angels motioned to a third nearby and then the three of them quickly walked off the platform they were on and disappeared out of view. Layla immediately turned and hurried back in to hiding with an excited smile on her face.

"Now we wait," said Layla

"You go girl!" said Samantha. "Nice work!"

The girls sat on the ground, out of view and waited. They heard lightning strike in the distance. Trinity had drawn her knees up to her chest and wrapping an arm around them she, rested her chin on one hand looking at the other two girls. Samantha started to draw shapes on the ground beside her as she waited. Layla stared out across the river, looking at nothing in particular, but listening to the waters as they flowed past. They waited for a few minutes saying nothing.

Suddenly Layla jerked her head up. "I hear someone approaching," she whispered.

Within moments a figure appeared and glanced at the girls. Seeming satisfied, he motioned to the other two angels. The girls immediately stood together apprehensively as three magnificent angels appeared towering over them. Layla was acutely aware that she and her friends were not of this world and almost felt that they were trespassing on foreign soil.

"Don't be afraid. We are here to help you. We had word that you would be coming," said one. "We will help you to get to the throne. My name is Shar, this is Seraph, and this here is Trillion."

Their friendly introduction broke the ice and alleviated her stress as Layla breathed out a sigh of relief.

"My name is Layla, this is Trinity and Samantha."

There wasn't much else to say. A regular surface greeting didn't seem appropriate. To ask how the angel's day was going, seemed a bit weird, so she just got to the point, "We will need to get past this crowd undetected."

"We can cloak you for short periods of time," said Shar. "In preparation for your arrival we figured out the best route to the throne. There will be places we can rest out of view, but you must be confident and full of faith for our cloaking to work."

The three girls each paired up with an angel. As Layla stood next to Trillion, she reminded herself of the fact that not so long ago she was sitting in her lounge room catching up on her devotional readings, or 'Devo's' as she would sometimes call them. Now she was standing next to an angel, about to walk into a spiritual palace, populated by angels and demons, and ready to do battle if required. 'I would never have imagined that my day would turn out like this! Whoever said Christianity was boring?!' she thought to herself.

18

REVISITED

- MISSION LIBERTY -

Liberty pushed herself as hard as she could. She sprinted away from the dragon and the demons that were in pursuit. The direction that the Holy Spirit had given her allowed her to focus on a destination. But the café was a long way off, and chances of outrunning her pursuers seemed slim. She didn't know what she would find at the café to help, but she had no other options.

***

On-surface Bethany was engrossed in watching a movie at home. Liberty was in danger and needed her friend to pray. The Holy Spirit prompted Bethany in his usual way, with a thought. Bethany frowned and continued watching the movie. The dragon rapidly approached Liberty. The gap was closing. Bethany brushed the thought away again as she sat in her comfortable armchair with the footrest up, enjoying her moment of solitude having spent the whole day with friends and family. Because the thought of Liberty continued to press her, she made a decision to include Liberty in her prayers just before she went to bed. This decision caused the prompting to drift away and give her peace. It wasn't so much that Bethany was directly disobeying the Holy Spirit, rather she didn't understand that some things required an immediate response. Time was running out, only moments left. If surface help did not come, Liberty would be wrenched out of the vision, have her body thrown onto the floor at home, and the mission would fail. The Holy Spirit called on Sarah, but Sarah had not yet trained herself to heed the Spirit's leading. The thought of Liberty drifted through her mind, but so did the thought of church the next day, seeing her friends and the horrible prospect of babysitting those troublesome twins next week.

Mr. Hoffman, the teacher who would let the girls have their Christian meeting in his classroom, was also watching TV that night and Liberty's name filled his thoughts. He immediately rose from his chair, turned to his wife and said, "Cup of tea love?"

"Sure," she responded, and Mr. Hoffman wandered into the kitchen. Liberty's name seemed to shout loudly at him as he turned on the jug and got two cups from the cupboard.

"Lord I pray that you would strengthen Liberty, protect her, keep her safe and give her wisdom and insight into whatever situation she finds herself in."

***

Those words were the immediate response that was needed. No sooner had the words left Mr. Hoffman's mouth, the power of them surged like an electric charge through Liberty's mind.

Liberty looked along the road to what lay ahead. As she did, everything in her immediate vicinity began to shift around her, and she found herself running through an optical tunnel with a crystal clear focal point at the far end. The scene formed in her mind like jigsaw pieces being drawn together into a three-dimensional model of her surroundings. She could suddenly see in front of her, to the side and behind her all at the same time as she continued to sprint toward her destination. Her legs were running automatically, moving as fast as they could. While she was running, her spirit was gathering the information from all around, forming a picture in her mind of who was chasing her and how close they were. She noticed small details. The demons were closing in. Information continued to be absorbed, 'Building, door, rubbish bin, drain, lamp-post, parked car, another demon off to her right turned and joined the chase. 'There... train track... train... train approaching... can shoot the gap.'

Liberty adjusted her course and ran towards the track. If she could get there fast enough, she could clear the front of the train before it passed. She put her life into her hands and sped toward the train as it came hurtling towards her. With all the energy she had, she dived for the gap, hands out directly in front of her. Time slowed, and she seemed to glide over an unnatural distance as the tracks passed below her. The train almost brushed her boots as it shot past. She landed safely on the opposite side in a roll to break her fall. The tumble on the ground took her back to her feet, and she continued to race. The demons were slowed down by the train which put more distance between herself and them. The dragon raged behind her. It swooped and drove its claws into the train, picking it up and flinging it across the street and into a row of shops on the other side of the square. Glass, chairs and window frames exploded onto the road.

***

The result of the derailment of the train and the carnage of its wake was manifested on the surface. Passengers on the surface felt the train jolt as the demon plunged its claws in to it. Though it was hurled away in the spirit, it remained on the tracks on the surface. Passengers saw nothing of the dragon, but the lurch caused a man, wearing a heavy brown jacket, to hit his head on the tubular steel bar that acted as a handhold for standing passengers. He spun his head around in anger to see if anyone had seen the incident. Three or four pairs of eyes glanced up.

"What are you all looking at?!" he shouted at the boy who was closest to him. More worried expressions turned to look. His knuckles turned white as he continued to tightly grip the handrail. His cheeks flushed under his long matted hair and he felt heat rise up from under his clothing. He spun around and pulled down the emergency brake and the train screeched to a halt. He forced the doors open and jumped out of the train. Tripping over, he sprawled on to the pavement. Patrons of the café looked in amazement as the train slid and shuddered along the tracks to a standstill. The man clumsily picked himself up, yelled some kind of unintelligible cry and ran off, pushing a couple out of the way who were about to enter a nearby shop.

***

While in the spirit realm, Liberty was unaware of how the pursuit was effecting the surface. Still on the run, Liberty felt that she could make it to the open doors of the café, but the glass frontage wasn't going to provide much protection from her pursuers. Surely the café wasn't her haven of refuge. She looked, ... tables... chairs... service door... no padlock... it's open!' As she neared the café, the service door to the side of the café appeared to be ajar.

'Glad it's not locked!' she thought. Feeling exhausted she made the last dash straight for the door. Grasping the handle, she flung it open and burst through. As the door swung open to its fullest extent, it then ricocheted back again and slammed shut. With the horde only seconds away, she noticed a lever to lock the door from the inside and slammed it down. 'Can demons transport themselves through walls and doors in this realm?' She stepped backward, eyes focused intently on the door. She drew out her sword and held it tightly in both hands with the tip extended out in front of her towards the door. The horde on the other side started to bang and claw on the door. That settled it in her mind, doors and walls set confines for them here just like they set boundaries for people on the surface. Liberty breathed in deeply and let out a sigh of relief. She backed away from the door, turned and quickly stepped down the flight of stairs before her.

Liberty felt safer now that she was underground. 'Surely that dragon can't follow me down here,' she thought. She was still breathing hard and fighting back the tears.

As she walked, she realised that she had the ability to see in the dark. Another reason to be thankful. She couldn't pinpoint any particular light source, but she could still pick out details around her.

There were all kinds of electrical boxes and valves to gas mains and sewage pipes lining the walls. Liberty's locator directed her to the right, but she could see no opening to the right. The corridor continued straight ahead for about twenty metres, then turned left. She continued to follow the corridor for a few minutes, then it opened out into a huge shaft. The shaft dropped away about three stories to a watery vault below, and a wire bridge hung, suspended across the expanse in front of her. The bridge connected the platform that she was standing on to the network of tunnels on the other side. She stepped out onto the suspension bridge.

Liberty walked carefully along the wire bridge, now quite disorientated as to where she was in relation to the surface because she was being directed away from where she wanted to go. She continued, hoping that she would soon be able to head in the direction that her locator was indicating.

Liberty got to the other side of the bridge and continued along one of the tunnels. A few metres in, she noticed a storm water drain off to her right. 'Wonder how far down it goes?' she thought, 'I don't want to go down too deep into the earth in case I can't get back up again, but it's leading in the right direction.' It was the more risky option, looking down into a tunnel with the end shrouded from view, but there was no point walking any further away from where she wanted to go. 'Lord, do I go?' No response. She opted to explore it and slid down the drain, landing with a splash to a lower level beneath the city. The large pillars that were part of the foundations of the city towered above her. Her eyes were drawn upwards to where they branched off at the top, creating interlocking patterns on the ceiling. Ribbons of light were dancing over the patterns on the stonework above her head, created by the ripples of the water below. The movement of the reflections seemed to bring to life the protrusions and recesses.

Suddenly she heard some loose rocks fall to her right and a scurrying of claws. Her dreams flooded back to her; she had been here before. Liberty remembered the sequence of events from her dream that were about to unfold. She didn't have to look this time but lunged to the left where she knew the platform to be. She then lunged a second time to escape the next blow, bracing herself for the impact against the wall. Her sword was knocked from her hand. She looked up at the demon. Is this the moment? The demon sword went up, not slowing down. In her spirit, she knew she had to move again. She still had energy, so she threw herself back to the right in a final attempt to escape. The blade struck concrete. A narrow miss. Liberty was now cornered, 'Isn't there supposed to be a wall of fire by now that destroys this demon?!' she thought in dismay. Liberty looked up through her strands of matted hair.

"Come on fire ball, where are you?!"

Flash! Explosion… blaze… heat… roar… echo… silence.
As her eyes readjusted, she saw the smoldering ruins around her. 'Talk about cutting it close!' she thought, catching her breath.

Liberty picked herself up, a bit sore after the knocks that she received on the hard stone. She rubbed her neck and arched her back to stretch it out. Liberty then pulled back her hair in a ponytail and wiped the sweat from her brow. 'Right!' she thought with determination, 'No more surprises. I'm going to be ready for the next dirty demon!' She puffed some loose hair that hung in front of her face out of the way.

"Lord, let's go!"

19

RASOR PEAK
- mission boys -

Exposed, the boys dangled from a single rope, suspended high above the ground. All around was quiet, apart from the wind gusts swirling about them. The sound of rope creaking under tension as it held their weight was the only other sound, like a flexing mast on high seas. The three looked out at the skies, scanning for signs of danger. As they looked to where the cloud cover thinned out, they could momentarily see grey shadows circling overhead. Caden felt nervous, at the mercy of the elements. The three lone figures were dangling high from a rope with nowhere to go but slowly upwards. Tristan's confidence dwindled the higher he got.

Suddenly the silence was broken. A fearsome screech echoed around the boys. The demons had been exercising self-restraint, waiting for the perfect opportunity to bring the onslaught, and now was the moment. A demon sharply turned and swooped in to intimidate them, stretching out its claws to swipe Tristan.

"Watch out, we are under attack!" shouted Tristan. Caden and Jack saw a dozen dragon-like creatures swooping and squawking like a hungry colony of scavenging vultures.

Jack quickly drew out his sword to fend off any that came near while he held the rock face with his other hand. Caden drew out an arrow, but instead of shooting, he instinctively raised it and plunged it into the cliff. Surprisingly, it readily penetrated the rock and firmly wedged itself in the face. Suddenly it thickened and tripled in size. 'I guess I picked the right one,' he thought. Using it as an anchor, Caden took the coil of loose rope that hung off his belt and tied himself to the arrow to secure his position on the cliff. Now that he was safely tied, it freed up both hands to retaliate. He drew the next arrow, placed it in his crossbow and fired it at a demon. The bow kicked back in his arm with remarkable force. The weapon was so powerful that he barely saw the arrow fly through the air before it pierced a demon causing it to burst into flames. The demon let out a long screech as it fell writhing through the air.

Caden was the only one with a long range weapon. He aimed and fired again, and another demon was taken out. This time as the arrow struck, the demon shattered to pieces like ice smashed with a hammer. Caden continued to take out demons with his crossbow. Another swooper hurtled towards Jack, colliding with him. The straps securing his shield broke as it slid off his back. The shield fell through the air, tossed about like a leaf in the wind, toward the ground below. Jack's body swung towards the cliff and bashed against the rock. He was knocked unconscious and grew limp. All the while, Tristan had continued to climb to get to the shelter of a cave so that he could help to pull his friends up. 'No point all of us being sitting ducks!' he thought.

Tristan made it to the cave and looked down. Caden was doing the best he could to shoot any of the swoopers that came into range.

Caden looked down at Jack and then looked up at Tristan. "Jack isn't moving, and I'm stuck," he yelled.

Tristan shouted back, "All I can do is help take some of the weight as you climb, but I can't pull you and Jack up by myself. You will both still have to climb to get out of danger."

"What can we do? Jack's out cold. We can't just leave him hanging there. We both need to pull him up somehow so that we can make the final ascent together."

The air filled with the noise of screeching echoing off the cliff face. Just then a swooper curved toward them and seizing the opportunity to pick off the weakest, flew straight for Jack. Its razor claws were outstretched, ready to tear at him.

Caden reached behind for another arrow, but it got caught in his quiver. He shouted in frustration, "What! Come on, get free!" The swooper went in for the kill and grabbed at Jack's leg and shoulders. The pain and tearing action ripped Jack back into consciousness. He let out a painful yell. The swooper tore free and circled around in preparation for a final attack.

"Jack!" yelled Caden. Jack looked up with pain in his eyes.

"I'm done," called Jack. "I've come as far as I can with you." With great effort, he drew his sword and raised it to the rope.

"No!" shouted Caden. "You can't! You will drop out of the vision, and we will lose."

"I can't climb anymore; I'm bleeding too much. I need to tell you something before I go. This quest isn't just a vision," Jack called out.

"What are you talking about?" shouted Caden. The situation was tense, and Caden was getting annoyed that Jack wasn't making sense.

"I was assigned to protect you. I'm sorry I couldn't see that through to the end. It was always going to be just the two of you in the end anyway. Don't give up, keep moving." Jack's sword rested on the rope, ready for a single slice. The swooper was already on its way back with claws open for a fresh attack.

"No!" yelled Caden in anguish, 'We can't do this without you."

"You must and you will!" he replied.

Just then another swooper appeared out of nowhere, lined up, and went in to attack Caden. Jack's eyes widened as he saw what was about to happen. With all his might, he flung his sword up at the incoming swooper, and the sword stuck fast in its chest. A cry echoed along the cliff face as the demon smashed into the rocks just below Caden's feet. It bounced off, and they watched it fall far below.

Jack looked over his shoulder, seeing his fate was imminent, pushed out from the cliff face with his legs, and guided the rope into the path of a claw. A sudden slackness recoiled through the rope. Tristan and Caden jolted as the weight was released. They looked down in disbelief watching Jack fall. As he did, he began to transform. Wings unfolded from his back and feathers tore free. He looked up, and as Caden and Jack's eyes met, in one last engagement, Caden realised he was not looking at a man. As Jack continued to fall, he faded into nothing.

"Deceived!" shouted the swooper, letting out an angry screech, realising that it had attacked an angel rather than a human. It stormed off to find reinforcements to finish off the other two.

"Tristan!" yelled Caden. "Jack was an angel!"

"A what? I can't hear you," responded Tristan.

"An angel!" Caden yelled again.

Suddenly the two felt more alone than ever.

"We need to move," said Tristan. "It was meant to be. Just you and me now. We can complete this together."

Caden untied himself from his anchor that was still holding fast in the cliff and gathered his strength to climb. Without the weight of Jack on the end of the rope, and with Tristan pulling him up from above, he found that he could continue. Caden got to the ledge that Tristan was on. They both forced themselves to continue, aiming for a better shelter that they could see in the rock above. They strained and groaned, with each movement as they continued to ascend the exposed face.

As the minutes slipped by, Caden tried to focus his thoughts on the handholds that were within reach. Slabs of rock jutted out giving opportune places to grip with his hands and clefts within the rock allowed resting places for his feet. But his thoughts drifted back to Jack as he considered the time that they had spent together. Caden searched in his memory looking for clues from past conversations with Jack that may have indicated he was an angel. He remembered the first meeting with Jack in the park. Caden remembered that Jack had said that he would have a significant impact in the city. 'He must have already known about the assignment,' thought Caden, also remembering that Jack had just vanished after their conversation. Caden had looked around, scanning the park from where he stood, but Jack seemed to have dissolved into the night. 'How was I supposed to know anyway?' Caden thought. 'I guess…' directing his thoughts toward God, 'it was for our good that we had Jack with us, but why didn't you let us know until now? I just assumed he was like us…' his thoughts then went down another tangent, "God, have I met other angels before?"

'What do you think?' came the response in his mind.

For Caden that was almost as good as a 'Yes.'

Caden dragged his thoughts back into the moment and looked up at Tristan who was making real progress. "Did you know Jack was an angel? Are you an angel too?" asked Caden

"No way! And no, I didn't know he was an angel either. All I know is that I am not surprised by anything in this place anymore." said Tristan.

The truth was that the two of them were tiring and finding it hard to keep going. Grasping each handhold became increasingly arduous than the previous. Tristan's arms were shaking, and he called out, "I'm really struggling. I'm feeling weak and finding it more and more difficult to find handholds. There seem to be fewer holds up here."

"How far do we have to our next shelter?" replied Caden

"Looks like it's about twenty metres up, but I can't see a path we can take to it. We may have to find another route," said Tristan.

"There must be a way. We can't start over," Caden responded.

"Watch out!!" yelled Caden. "Another swooper!"

"We're like sitting ducks up here. God, help us!" Caden called out.

Three swoopers rounded the cliff face for another attack.

20

CLOAKED
- mission girls -

Trinity leaned into Shar as he spread his cloak around her. His cloak did not conceal her entirely but would be enough to cloak her presence from the unsuspecting enemy. But, if a demon took a particular interest, there would be little to stop her from being discovered.

Trinity felt excited and privileged being this close to an angel.

'I wonder if anyone in the whole world has ever been this close to an angel before,' she thought. She could sense no heartbeat or any warmth coming from him, just the presence of the silky fabric draped over her body.

'Doing this is actually quite nuts!' she said to herself. 'But awesome too!' she thought with a smile. 'I'm sure this plan will work. Lord, you have brought us this far. Right now we are in the middle of your will. The throne is our mission, and we shall get there!' she thought resolutely.

Trinity was out in front. The others followed behind. She gazed along the road ahead. It seemed like an endless distance to the entrance of Grace Falls. 'Once we get to the entrance, then what? Do we just walk right up to the throne? Okay, stop over-thinking. One challenge at a time. Let's just get ourselves to the entrance and perhaps there we can find a place to regroup and prepare ourselves to enter the falls.'

Trinity saw two of the enemy standing beside the river from a distance, but now they were rapidly approaching them, up ahead on the left.

"Are you alright?" asked Shar in a hushed tone.

"Yes," responded Trinity.

"Good. Keep your head straight. Don't look down and don't look at them. They can sense someone looking at close-range," Shar instructed.

Trinity thought it would have been better for her to lower her head to conceal herself more, but she obeyed and looked straight ahead. She pressed herself against her angel. 'Shar could take these two demons on with no problems,' thought Trinity. 'But, I guess the longer we can conceal our presence, the longer we can put off an all-out war.'

As the pair came within metres of the demons, the demons shuffled backward to maintain enough clearance between themselves and the angel. Trinity's heart beat faster. She looked straight ahead and kept on walking. The others also passed by the demons who continued to talk with each other, not paying too much attention to the three angels who were passing them. Trinity had not turned to look back but trusted that the others were following and hoping they were feeling undaunted. As Trinity got to a place amongst the rocks where she was safely out of view, she turned to look for the others behind her. But Trinity had a moment of worried confusion. She expected to see four figures following, but she could only see two figures walking alone. She saw the two angels, but not her friends.

'What happened? They've gone!' thought Trinity.

"Where are they?!" Trinity whispered.

"Your friends? That's them," he said. "When I cloaked you, my form became your garment. You walked clothed in my form. You looked like an angel walking alone. When an enemy looks at you, all they will see is one of us. The danger is in making eye contact. Only through your eyes is your true identity revealed. We cannot cloak the eyes. Your eyes are windows to what is really there."

As she looked, she saw that it was Samantha walking and Layla following behind, looking as stately and as regal as angels. She could distinguish them now, by their faces. Her friends looked amazing, like princess warriors returning to take up their residence at Grace Falls.

Once the three of them were safely behind the rocks, the girls stepped out from under the angels, and they became six distinct entities again.

"Great!" said Layla. "We can go right through like this."

"We could," said Trillion, "but there are many enemies to pass. We have now made it to the base of Grace Falls and the gateway of the palace. The next part is harder to get through. The entrance opens out into the main foyer. This foyer is always densely populated. There will be a lot of enemies to navigate through, and they are heightened in their alertness because they are aware of the importance of this juncture in time. It is also wise to conceal our presence from other angels so as not to draw attention to ourselves. The fewer who know you are here, the better. When you enter through the gates, you will see an archway slightly to your right, on the opposite side of the foyer. You will begin by walking straight into the foyer. When you get about halfway through, veer to the right and aim for that archway. There will be no place to rest. You will continue under the archway and into the Hall of Coronation. The hall will also have a lot of activity, but there are no gatherings scheduled for the next few hours, which is good news for us because we wouldn't be able to get through a formal meeting of council. At the opposite end of the hall is the central staircase. Once we reach the stairs, I do not know what will happen because we may not be able to continue to hold our 'cloak' without a rest. I'm hoping that once we get there, we will get some help from the surface."

"What do you mean by help from the surface? What will happen if we don't get help?" asked Trinity.

"We operate through the prayer and faith of believers. If we don't get support, the enemy gains the upper hand. We need help from the surface because Satan got control of the world way back in the Garden of Eden. The ground became cursed, and Satan obtained dominion. But there is a greater authority that can be claimed by believers who extend the Kingdom of Heaven on earth through faith. We work through partnership and don't operate alone.

"Partnerships for assignments usually begin with a prompting that heaven releases. The Holy Spirit will prompt a single believer to pray, or the Holy Spirit may ask many Christians to intercede. They will exercise their free will to pray, or not. In our present situation, if we don't get an engagement of faith from the surface, our cloaks may fade, our cover will disappear and we will either have to flee or fight or both."

"Well, why doesn't God just clear the way for us?" Trinity questioned again.

"Because the currency of heaven is 'faith.' God doesn't break his laws and rules that he has set to govern all things. He doesn't need to because they are perfect." Trillion paused. "I can explain more, but time is short, we have talked long enough. Come, we must go."

***

Meanwhile, on the surface, Drake called an emergency meeting. Even though he wasn't mayor yet, he still held some degree of influence with various members of the council. It was an unusual time to meet on Saturday night, but Drake was infuriated that a Christian crusade was going ahead in the middle of the city for the whole of next week. The Christians also didn't inform the transport authority about the congestion that it would cause. The four council members sat around a table with demons perched on each of their high-back chairs, unseen by the men. The beast's claws sank deep into the leather, and they permeated the room with the foul odour of deception.

"Those Christians think they can do whatever they want. We can't let them cause chaos in downtown mid-week. Give them Sundays, but not mid-weeks too!" bellowed Drake.

"It's outrageous! They don't have consent," said Portman.

"Well actually, they do have consent," said Chester holding up a document. "The whole thing went on file a month ago, and when we took our time in responding, Linda, I think her name is, came in herself last week. But I sent her away empty-handed promising that I would get the final signature she needed. In truth, it only needs the one signature, but I'm with you about these Christians wanting to run public events."

"So she doesn't have the document?" asked Drake.

"Nope, this is it," Chester replied.

"No other copies anywhere?" Drake questioned.

"The only one," smiled Chester holding it up, "and I may well misplace it in the shredder."

"Great! That was easy." Drake stood to leave, "We're done here."

"What's that smell?" said Phillips who hadn't spoken much during the exchange.

"Don't know. I like it! Thank you, gentlemen," said Drake as he walked out of the room. Wafts of deception continued to permeate where they had met.

As the men were leaving the four demons, half smiled, half sneered at each other.

"Go and report it," said one demon to the other, "and don't mess it up, you fool."

The creature growled and rose to leave. As it rose, its claws tore more of the leather. The leather on the backs of all the chairs had criss-crossed claw marks all over them; evidence of many a council meeting. The slashes in the backrests weren't visible to the natural eye. Though, if someone knew what they were looking for and were in tune with spiritual things, they might be able to detect faint markings. Just as the eyes are windows to the soul, so too are they outward windows, giving a person the ability to see much of the spiritual landscape, even though overlaid by the natural.

***

This meeting was bad timing for the girls who were preparing to walk the gauntlet of angels and demons through the foyer. The three girls concealed themselves in their angelic cloaks and quickly stepped out into the open. They moved promptly towards the entrance. Just then, four angels emerged, walking towards them.

Trinity, who was out in the lead, looked straight ahead. The four seemed to be on assignment with a look of resoluteness on their faces. As Trinity passed the closest one, the angel turned to look at her. Trinity maintained her gaze straight ahead. She kept walking, using all her willpower not to turn and look at the angel. She heard no commotion behind, but remained on edge with a heightened sense of awareness, hoping that Samantha and Layla would follow suit.

The three came to the gates and passed under the high canopy of carved stone. Six large pillars on each side, stretching from floor to ceiling, lined the wide opening. It looked like a structure from ancient Rome, but with the touch of the divine. It was a thrill to be walking through such a magnificently crafted environment. Samantha allowed herself a quick glance up at the magnificent architecture. She couldn't help but be captivated by the divine craftsmanship. 'I suppose all man-made structures have the touch of the divine,' she thought. 'We're made in the image of God after all. This whole place seems to be perfect in design and form.'

The foyer was a throng of angelic and demonic beings. Trinity focussed with determination as she saw the challenge before her. The girls each, in turn, crossed the threshold and stepped out into the crowd, heading straight for the centre of the foyer. Trinity maintained her straight path adjusting her speed to slow down or move more quickly so as to avoid bumping into anyone. She found it hard to judge distance because all was a wash of movement around her. After some time she thought, 'Am I in the centre of the room yet?' She realised as she walked that she lost all sense of time. She had no idea how long she had been walking. 'Have I just started or have I been going for ages? I must be about in the middle by now.' She scanned for the archway and caught sight of it over to her right and adjusted her course directly towards it. Trinity looked dead-ahead, avoiding eye contact with any being at all costs.

Samantha could feel a trickle of perspiration running down her neck and back. She also realised that she had been holding her breath. As Samantha walked, her breathing settled into an even rhythm. Getting almost halfway through the foyer, she noticed that some demons shuffled out of the way as they came into proximity. All the beings seemed to be pre-occupied on their missions and especially the angels.

When Layla, who was last of the three, got half way through the room, something terrible happened. As she looked over toward the archway on her right, she was unintentionally jostled by a demon on her left, who shoved her into the path of another demon. The collision knocked her off balance, and she took a couple of steps backward. The demon immediately hissed at her, giving her a huge fright. She raised her right hand up to eye level, shielding her eyes from looking at the creature. The demon hissed again. She drew her sword and gripped it tightly in her left hand, but kept it low to the ground so as not to directly challenge the demon, rather warn it to keep its distance. Angels and demons stopped in their tracks and turned to look. Tension filled the air around her. She slowly lowered her arm and her gaze to avoid catching anyone's eye. All she could see were legs, boots and the hems of robes. Her friends were now far ahead, not daring to look back at the commotion behind them. She could see some of the angels nearby place their hands on the hilts of their swords, ready to draw.

'This is intense,' she thought in a mild state of panic, 'God, I'm going to lose this.' She stood, immersed in the situation, unable to run, unable to look, unable to think. Just then a portion of the Bible came to her mind. She remembered Peter walking on water. He began well, but then he started to sink because he realised that he was doing the impossible, walking on water. But the truth was that Peter wasn't walking on water, he was walking on a miracle. In the midst of the miracle, he lost focus and looked around him and could only see the water. The waves intimidated him, and Peter began to sink. He cried out to Jesus to save him. Jesus caught his hand, raised him up out of the water, and walked back with him the rest of the way. She was now in the same dilemma. She had been walking in the miracle, but now the situation overwhelmed her.

Layla whispered, "Jesus, save me."

21

UNDERGROUND
- mission liberty -

Liberty decided to walk around the perimeter of the open area, staying close to the walls, rather than walking through the water. At least that way she had the wall as protection and wouldn't have to defend on all sides from an attack.

As she walked, she raised her arm towards the wall and held out her hand, running her fingers along the stonework. As she did, she noticed inscriptions engraved into the stone. They were all written in some angelic language. She studied them as she walked and discovered that she could read what they said.

The first title read: 'Francis Martin – 1964 - founded 'The Life & Health Centre.'

Below was the inscription: 'As Mayor of the city and a devoted believer in Jesus Christ, Francis Martin, using personal funds, founded 'The Life & Health Centre' to provide healthcare and mentorship for troubled youth. This centre helped hundreds of young people find their way back to a healthy lifestyle, positive outlook on life, and many opportunities that propelled them into their calling. In particular Kenny Dorsa, who at age eight was caught breaking-and-entering, and by fourteen was wanted for more serious crimes. Within ten years of being taken in by the Centre, he became one of the most effective church leaders that this city has ever seen.'

'What a powerful testimony,' thought Liberty. Revelation rolled into her mind, 'These are the stories and acts of many people, recorded on stone, making up the foundations of this city.'

Each inscription was a moment in time, engraved on a single block, memorialised as an instance when a person did something so significant that it shaped the future of the city. These blocks were all around her holding up Riverdale. Having noticed the ones next to her, she looked around as far as the eye could see and saw that every single block that made up the foundations had an inscription on it. 'These are amazing snapshots of history. I must have time to read a couple more,' she thought.

Title: Amber Burgess – 1992 – Began Full-Vert.

Mother of four began an outreach to the skateboarding community called 'Full-Vert.' Amber saw an opportunity for the ministry because her son had a passion for skateboarding. Amber set up outreaches, competitions, and exhibitions featuring famous Christian skateboarders. Within the first two years, she found herself with twenty-five volunteers, many of whom had become Christians under her ministry. A further fifty skateboarders had also become Christians through Full-Vert outreaches.

Title: George Stone – 1943 – Lived for Christ

He gave his life for the cause of the Gospel.

'That one is short. I guess God knows what he did and probably God is the only one who needs to know the details.' Liberty began to think about the stories of people who had given their lives for the cause of Christ. 'The blood and the sacrifice of many individuals,' she mused. Liberty felt a renewed surge of purpose, 'I must complete my mission. These people have not given their lives in vain.'

Liberty picked her way around the perimeter, staying close to the wall. There were various platforms to navigate and loose rock in places. Every so often she would stop and listen. The background sound of dripping and distant rumbling noises of what sounded like cars driving overhead, but she heard no other signs of life.

'No other signs of life,' came a whisper beside her. 'No other signs of life,' she thought. Her footing started to slip on the gravel. She frantically reached out her arms for something to steady herself. There was nothing to anchor her. She reached out in vain, only to grasp handfuls of air. Her boots continued to slide on the gravel as if she was on the edge of some steep mountain about to fall into a deep ravine.

"What's going on?!" she cried out in a moment of panic. One last slide on the gravel caused the earth to fall away, and Liberty fell into blackness. Nothing but darkness surrounded her. Though she was rapidly descending through some massive expanse, still reaching out as far as she could for anything to hold on to, she felt no rush of air from below that one would expect as she fell. Liberty realised that she no longer had any kind of falling sensation, it was more like floating in an endless sea. She hung suspended, in empty space, between nowhere and somewhere else. She realised that she felt eternally distanced from life and any other person. She was alone, an immeasurable distance from the surface. Her soul had slipped into a lifetime of solitude.

'It's only a lifetime,' she thought, shrouded in depression. Liberty looked out at nothing; all was empty, a relational being without a single soul aware of her existence. She reached out her hands for something to touch, but still, they waved through emptiness.

"I am without hope. I am without life," she said. As she floated in space, she drew her knees up close to her chest into a foetal position and waited for nothing in particular. Then, after an undetermined length of time, her mind embraced a single spark originating from her spirit. The spark rose like a glowing ember in the midst of the darkness.

"What is that? It's a little spark. Where did that come from?" she pondered. 'It's like a tiny fiery flower with flaming petals that enlarge like flames and then retract again. It moves like it is alive. It is so beautiful; it gives me hope,' she thought with a smile.

"Without hope? No, that's not right," she corrected, "I have hope, I have life." Within the depths of her spirit, she felt the small warm glow of presence of God. It was distant, but it was there. As she focused on the spark within, on the hope, the spark flickered brighter, and she felt the warmth.

Then a rush of anger erupted from within her, "I'm being deceived," she yelled out. "Get me out of here!"

Suddenly the blackness receded in all directions. The deception ended and she returned to where she had been standing. Her feet were planted firmly on the gravel and beside her stood a demon shrouded in a cloak holding a vase. A white mist was rising from the vase, intoxicating the air around her. Immediately Liberty, with an angry growl and teeth gritted, sliced her blade upwards through the air, relieving the demon of its life. As the beast fell, she brought her sword around and slashed it again. This time the demon was sliced completely in half, and the remains of it fell onto the stones at her feet. The vase fell from its hand and smashed on to the ground, spilling its milky contents all over the gravel. A cloud from the substance that was inside the vase hung around her ankles like dry-ice. Momentarily the demon lay lifeless, then dissolved in a pool of bubbling acid. The cloaked figure faded into nothingness and the air around her head cleared.

'That was horrible,' she thought as tears began to fill her eyes. She brushed them away. 'Totally unexpected! God, please make me aware of the different attacks of my enemy.'

The Holy Spirit spoke to her spirit, 'I am always with you. I have given you gifts and abilities, but don't even trust in those. Trust in me and acknowledge me in all things and I will make your paths straight.'

Liberty barely understood what had just happened, but now realised that fulfilling her quest would require complete trust in the Lord.

'There is a lesson in everything,' she thought, 'On this spiritual plane which I find myself on, there is a battle to be fought with the blade in my hand and also with the thoughts of my mind. Teach me to maintain my focus on you, Lord.'

22

ice

- mission boys -

Pastor Shearman had a busy day, having led an extended staff meeting and making three pastoral visits. He arrived back at the church to finish off a couple of emails and to pray out the day. He felt the prompting of the Lord to go into the sanctuary. Shearman loved to go into the main auditorium of the church when no one else was there. Tomorrow it would be jam-packed for three services, but right now it was quiet, and there was always a sense of the presence of the Lord in that place.

Shearman stepped on to the stage and gazed out over the empty seats. He felt honoured to be in full-time ministry, serving the people that God had given him. The church had started as a small house group that he had been asked to lead. Before too long, the house became too small to hold such meetings, and four of them decided to rent the local hall each week and call it 'church.' From there, 'the rest is history,' so they say. The church grew to over 500 in five years, and due to an offer of land, Shearman decided it was time to build their building. Now, two years on from the completion of that project, he had his sights set on building another facility closer to the middle of town where he knew the ministry would continue to expand and grow.

As Shearman stood, sensing the presence of the Lord, he looked across to the keyboard that was on the left side of the stage. He decided to play a few notes.

Shearman was a seasoned keyboardist. When the church started, back in the early days, he would do everything. After setting up the chairs and greeting people at the doors, he would lead the worship, read out the notices and preach the sermon. These days, because he had built a great leadership team around him who were all gifted in their various roles, he was able to focus more on what he wanted to do which was to preach and to strategise about the direction of the church. It had been two years since he had lead worship.

As he played a worshipful tune, Tristan's face flashed across his mind. Tristan was an active member of his church, looking after the youth and half a dozen small groups. Shearman had also invited him to speak a few times at their youth conferences.

He felt compelled to pray for Tristan. As he worshipped, he prayed the blessing, protection, and anointing of God over Tristan's life. Caden's face also flashed across his mind. Caden was a part of the worship team and played guitar most Sundays.

'I better get serious,' Shearman thought, 'There may be a whole lot of people the Holy Spirit wants me to pray for tonight.'

In recent years Shearman had received revelation on prayer. His prayer had changed from offering up pleading kind of prayers to making declarations and proclamations instead. As he studied prayer, through reading the Bible, he received revelation that if he declared truth over a situation rather than pleading with God to change it, that it was more effective in partnering with God to achieve his purposes.

"I declare victory over Tristan and Caden in Jesus name. I pray that you would use both these boys mightily in days to come. Fill them Holy Spirit with your power and equip them to be victorious over every challenge that they face. Let them see your glory, Lord. Open their eyes to see their situation as you see. Fill their mind with your Word. Fill their heart with faith. Fill them to overflowing so that the very atmosphere around them changes. I declare your kingdom to be established in the environment around them and also in their hearts. Grant them victory and an overcoming Spirit I pray. In Jesus Name, Amen."

As Shearman prayed, he closed his eyes and tilted his head heavenward. The moment he raised his head, beams of glory shot straight up around him, unseen by him but perfectly visible in the spirit realm. Shearman's 'prayer-form', the visual substance of his prayer, was powerful and had authority. The glory resembled solid shafts of ice that rose up from the ground and reached high into the sky. All around was like a growing and expanding glass castle, refracting the background light. The sound of ice and glass sliding against each other rang out into the sky like sharpening a sword before a battle. As Shearman continued to pray, from the sides of the shafts, icy wings protruded and stretched outwards and upwards. All was in motion around him. Shafts and wings raised to the heavens. Sharp contrasts of icy blue highlights and deep blue hues glided across surfaces as the structures reflected off each other and continued to move and grow. None of this was visible with the natural eye, but in the spirit, all was alive with the power of prayer.

As the shafts reached cloud height, pieces broke off into sharp spear-like shards of glass. Each spear had a set of wings. The icy spears peeled off the main shaft and flew toward Razor Peak. A shower of spears and wings rushed toward their target. Icy trails blazed through the heavens like meteors forming blue trails of ice and dust.

***

Caden yelled out, "Tristan, look to the sky!"

As Tristan adjusted his gaze to look beyond the swoopers and into the distance, he saw a long thin cloud, glistening and glinting in the over the horizon. A strip of the sky appeared to have sprinkles of silver glitter. Whatever the sparkles were, they were coming nearer, and quickly. Then in no time at all, like a fleet of jet planes roaring past at low altitude, a shower of glass and ice slammed into the rock face. The whole rock face shuddered. It left both boys breathless. The shards penetrated deep into the rock and held fast. Shards pierced and sliced through the winged demons. Screeches and gurgling noises came from the throats of dying creatures. The thud of bodies slamming against the rock could be heard above and below them. Tristan closed his eyes tightly and hugged the side of the cliff, pressing his body as hard as he could into the rock. The pounding of ice smashing into the rock face vibrated his chest. The rock beneath his hands shuddered with the multiple impacts. Swoopers, which moments before had been preparing for an attack, were now pinned to the cliff face and slowly dissolving away into nothingness. None of the shards hit the boys, though some struck dangerously close.

Eventually, the impacts stopped. High up on the cliff face, still stunned by what had happened, the boys opened their eyes and looked around. A gentle breeze cooled the sweat on their faces. Caden's eyes began to sting as droplets of sweat soaked through his eyelashes. All was dead silent compared to the thunderous noise just moments ago. The onslaught of glass and ice had cleared the skies of all demons.

The boys remained still for a while. Then Tristan reached out to his left hand to grasp a shard of ice. It was tightly lodged and would not budge. Calculating that it could hold his weight, he hoisted himself up onto it to relieve his aching limbs. Another shard was fixed a little above Caden's head. Reaching out his right hand, then his left, he pulled himself up onto it. Both sat and looked at each other.

"Ha. Someone is looking after us," said Tristan with a smile and look of relief.

"Yeah, and I'm glad whoever sent those killer ice spears is a good shot because they are deadly!" said Caden.

"You know it!" Tristan agreed with a chuckle.

After sitting and looking at each other for a minute or so, Tristan said, "We can make that shelter now, plenty of handholds. Let's go."

As the two climbed, using the shards as handholds and footholds, they found the climbing much easier. Once they reached the shelter, they decided only to rest for a few minutes and then make the final push to the top. The highest concentration of shards was now below them, but a few had struck higher up and would help them get to the summit.

The climb was long, and sweat was pouring off them by the time they were within reach of the top. At the summit was a ledge with an overhang where the boys could hide under to get some shelter. They rested for a while to catch their breath.

"Hardest climb ever," said Tristan.

Caden, still recovering from their ordeal, remained silent.

From their vantage point, Tristan looked across the city and realised he could see Grace Falls. "Lord, help the girls and help us," he prayed.

Eventually, Caden, who was thinking of Jack asked, "Do you think angels can die?"

"No, they go on for eternity like us. Spirits can't die, they are spiritual beings," Tristan replied. "The question is where do they go? Death is not something that happens at the end of life, 'Death' is a place. Death has a location, and I can tell you confidently that Jack isn't there." There was a pause. "Just as death is not the end of life, life isn't a beginning either, or even a 'state.' 'Life' in essence is a person. To be with him is to be in Life," finished Tristan.

"Where do you get that stuff!" said Caden with a smile. "You have got some sweet revelation going on. But I just wish I knew where Jack is now, and what it means when an angel falls in battle here. Do you know that too?"

"If we are supposed to know, I guess we'll find out eventually," said Tristan thoughtfully.

"I'm taking a look over the edge to see what's up there," said Caden after a few more minutes. Caden wriggled his way up and into a viewing position and carefully peered over the top of the ledge to survey the summit of Razor Peak.

23

OPENINGS
- mission Liberty -

Echoes of what had just happened to Liberty continued to influence her emotions. She felt lost in some dungeon, alone and forgotten about, far below the surface, untouched by sunlight. But she knew that she wasn't alone. She knew that the Lord was watching her, that he loved her and that he was the one who had assigned her this mission. But, she still found the need to fight the feeling of isolation that welled up within her.

'Why do I need to be alone God? Why can't I do this with friends?' The reply came, 'Each person has a different journey to take. No one can take it for you. Do not compare your path to someone else's. Everyone has personal battles to fight and victories to win.' The response comforted Liberty a little because she knew this to be true, so she pressed on with renewed determination.

Up ahead, the passageway ended at a wall. Rungs protruded from the wall, leading up to a circular hatch in the ceiling. There seemed to be no other option but climb the ladder and try to open the hatch. Once Liberty reached the top of the ladder, she braced herself against it and pressed her palm on the hatch above and pushed. The heavy lid was hinged on one edge and lifted slightly. As she pushed with all her strength, the rounded metal plate rose. The silence that she had got used to dissipated and her ears became filled with humming and rumbling sounds like engines and machinery in operation.

'Better be alert,' she said to herself. 'Sounds like we have some action up here.'

She pushed the hatch to open to its fullest extent, allowing it to fall away under its weight, and she hoisted herself up through the opening. Liberty found herself in amongst some metal boxes and machine parts, in the corner of a room. Remaining crouched, staying out of sight, she gently lowered the hatch into the closed position. She then slowly raised herself high enough to be able to see over the boxes. She saw what seemed to be a large service area as big as a warehouse. There were machines with pipes running through them, and lots of cabling ran along the walls and floor. The machines looked like they regulated whatever was flowing through the pipes.

Liberty thought, 'Seems like the water, electricity, and gas supply to the city runs through here.' There were also tanks with dials and valves protruding from them. A humming noise reverberated around the instruments. Some of the valves were open, releasing pressure from the lines. The hissing of gas mingled with the sound of the humming.

'Better stay away from that gas,' she thought, not liking the idea of choking to death. The plumes of gas rose from vents like smoky trees rising from an underground landscape. Of all the places she had been so far, this room seemed the most alive. Sounds of creaking pipes could also be heard overhead as heated gas rushed through them.

Liberty also noticed dull flickering lights in the room. These downlights illuminated what looked like control panels with screens displaying maps and information. Then she got a fright when one of the machines jerked. 'That's not a machine, that's a demon!'

To her horror, she realised these were workstations for demons. Demons were sitting in front of the screens, intent on what they were observing. She hadn't noticed them before because they sat so still with minimal movement. They were bony and scaly creatures and their exo-skeletal bodies seemed to blend into their surroundings. The room which initially emanated a low friendly hum, now took on a whole new evil as she realised it was a demon control room. As she gazed out from her vantage point, she saw the network of workstations with various instruments, with many demons sitting at them. She could just make out one of the screens. It looked like it was connected to surveillance equipment.

'They're probably spying on people, then communicating with other demons, helping them do their dirty work,' she thought. The thought of being watched made her angry, and she wished she could jump out and start relieving the demons of their posts, but Liberty knew that there were too many and that it was best to lower herself down through the hatch and leave as quietly as she had come.

As she reached for the hatch, she heard the Holy Spirit say, "Liberty."

"What!" she whispered in a frustrated tone. She had already decided it was no good trying to get through such a populated environment and was intent on getting back down to the quieter tunnel before being discovered. But she got the feeling that God was directing her to do just the opposite.

"God, if you want me to get through here, I'm going to need a little help!" She rose again and took another look at her surroundings.

She realised that she had only been looking at eye level and had neglected to lift her gaze. As she looked up for the first time, she saw gangways above her. She had far more chance of getting to the other side of this busy hub from up there. There were many demons scattered over the floor with no real clear path through. But from above, only a few demons were operating the elevated stations. There was also a central gangway that the others merged into which made a clear path to the other side of the room. But from up there she would be seen for sure.

"What do I do?" Liberty asked.

'You can't do this alone. You will need to trust my leading,' said the voice.

It seemed like God had a plan, which was reassuring.

"Okay, if you say so. Show me where to go," Liberty responded.

She looked for a way up to the top gangways. There were a few ladders situated around the room. Some were in the middle of the room, connecting the lower level to the upper level. The closest one to her wasn't far away, but she would need to get past two or three demon stations to get there.

She was about to make her way to the closest one on her hands and knees, when she heard someone beside her say, "Wait!"

In fright, she immediately rolled away and kicked in the direction of the voice.

"Careful!" the voice whispered.

"You be careful! I'll slash you in half if you sneak up on me like that!" she hissed, realising it was an angel who had come to her aid.

Liberty calmed down, and found her manners, "Sorry, thanks. Look, I need to get out of here, it's not safe. How do I get out?"

The angel smiled, "Don't get too excited. We have been dispatched to get you through the control centre of Riverdale. There are many of us here. We can jump you short distances, but won't be able to get you to all the way up a ladder to the top level, so you will need to climb. Even though the distance is too big to jump, you should still be fine to get to the top unseen. Watch that ladder over there."

The angel pointed to one of the freestanding ladders not far from where she was. As she looked, she saw a jet of gas shoot out from one of the valves, completely engulfing the ladder.

'Great! Now I have to climb through gas? Might conceal me long enough for the climb though, as long as I don't suffocate half way up!' she thought.

"Over here," the angel said. Liberty crawled over to where the angel was indicating. "I can give you a clear jump between here and that alcove over there. The angel drew out his sword and slashed it through the air, slicing that fabric of the atmosphere and opening up a tunnel to jump through.

"Go," the angel said. Liberty readied herself into a crouch position and then dived through the opening and immediately found herself rolling into the alcove. She looked back. The opening had closed, and the angel was about ten metres behind her, where she had been.

'Wow! That was incredible! A series of jumps like this could get me through,' she thought. She looked ahead to where she might jump to next. Another angel appeared beside her.

"Ready?" he said.

"Yes, ready to go again," Liberty responded.

"Over there, see where those three pipes are coming out of the ground? You won't be able to stay there long before your next jump." The angel was right. There was a demon sitting right at her landing spot with its back turned, intent on its work.

"We are going to open up two jumps for you at the same time."

Again Liberty got herself ready. The angel slashed an opening. Liberty braced herself, then pushed off with her legs and leaped through the opening. As she rolled onto the floor space in front of her, she bumped the chair which had a demon perched on it, busily working away. She immediately got up and dived through the other opening that another angel had already made for her. The creature broke its attention away from its work. It spun around on the chair. Angry red eyes looked around the floor and the immediate vicinity.

Another demon that was standing off to the side yelled, "Get back to it! Stop slacking off." Seeing nothing out of the ordinary, it returned to its work, mumbling something under its breath.

'That was close,' Liberty thought. 'One more jump should do it to get to that ladder. Where's my next angel?'

"Here," said a deep voice beside her.

"What do I do when I get to the top of the ladder? It looks pretty exposed up there."

"We haven't figured that out yet. I suggest you run for it and we will do what we can."

Liberty composed herself and got ready. The angel slashed an opening, and she dived through. Liberty found herself at the base of the ladder. She waited in a crouch position until the next release of gas. A burst of gas hissed out above her, and she quickly scaled the ladder. Liberty held her breath as she climbed. There was no point having her eyes open either. She wouldn't have been able to see anything in the midst of the cloud anyway. Liberty anticipated where the rungs would be and climbed blindly as fast as she could.

The gas was cold and filled her ears with hissing. She finally grasped at nothing and realised she had made it to the top of the ladder. She lifted herself up and rolled over onto the metal grate suspended above the many working demons. No one had seen her, so she picked herself up and started to walk quickly along the gangway. With so much noise around there was no need to be silent, so she maintained her quick pace. Liberty saw a demon walking along another gangway parallel to hers with a clipboard in hand looking at the details on it. It glanced up and spotted her.

"Ahhh!" it yelled out. Another couple of demons looked up and stood to their feet as they saw Liberty hurrying.

"Go, go, go!" said an angel beside her. As she ran, the suspended walkway trembled. Other angels were dispatched and appeared at various points along the gangway.

Demons started to occupy other walkways that connected to hers. The demons rushed towards Liberty, clambering over each other, trying to get to her first. As she ran, she heard a series of slams behind her getting closer to where she was. A series of barricades had been activated and were falling from the ceiling. A barrier started to fall in front of her. 'I'm trapped!' her mind yelled. But an angel appeared in front of her with raised arms to keep it open for a moment longer as she rolled under it.

Many barriers were slamming closed in an attempt to trap her on the gangway. Up ahead a barricade fell, blocking her way, but an angel sliced the air in front of it, and she ran through and appeared on the other side.

Demons were getting closer, but an angel blocked every lunge made by a demon. More angels appeared at the points along the gangway where others connected to the one that she was running on. Angels wielded swords holding back three or four demons at once. Liberty was running the gauntlet. More enemies were called to mount their attack on the girl who by now almost seemed smothered in darkness. The demons beneath her were in an uproar and as many pairs of eyes angrily watched her progress. The end was too far away.

Suddenly an angel larger than the others appeared in front of her carrying a javelin similar to the one that the angel had on the rooftop where they were shown the vision within the vision. He threw it, and it split the realm in front of her. Two other angels pulled back the curtains of her current reality, and she dived through.

This time, instead of being instantly translated to a place a few metres ahead of her, she found herself gliding through an open expanse that the atmospheric rupture had produced. She momentarily left the control room behind her and had entered an entirely different universe between her entry point and the exit point up ahead. All around her was silence. As Liberty glided through space, which had opened up around her, she saw countless stars. This in-between universe had millions of sparkling pinpoints of light set against a deep dark red backdrop.

'It's beautiful!' she thought. It was the birthplace of a galaxy. The stars were suspended within clouds of gas, spanning light-years across the heavens. Silhouetted against the glowing clouds were dark spheres and disc-like objects that she assumed could be planets and worlds, hung in space, perhaps waiting to be inhabited. There wasn't much time to admire her peaceful surroundings, or even make sense of what she was looking at because within seconds she was through and bracing herself to roll again on to the hard metal grate on the other side.

As she came out of the place in-between, she found that she had landed a long way ahead, at the end of the gangway. The danger seemed to be behind her. She quickly gathered her thoughts and got her legs moving again. Liberty ran out of the control room and into another tunnel.

A loud noise echoed around her as an angel slammed the door of the control room behind and stood guard. A dozen other angels appeared, to protect her from any demons that may try to force their entry through the door. Liberty quickly turned her head around to catch a glimpse of them. She then turned back and proceeded forward into the darkness ahead.

24

ORB

- mission girls -

On the surface, Linda, whom Layla had met with the day before at the planning meeting for the crusade, was still at the church working late. Linda was the one who had requested a project manager to help in the lead up to the event. Layla was selected to take on the role, not only because she was a qualified Project Manager, but also she was the daughter of the evangelist who was coming to town.

Linda looked over her papers again, triple checking that everything had been signed off.

'Where's that transport approval?' she thought to herself as she shuffled through her papers. Her heart sunk. 'I don't have it!' she thought in a mild state of panic. Trying to recount her steps, 'I went to the meeting… and he never gave it to me! He said it needed another signature and he still hasn't sent it through. If we get any resistance, I have no legal way of being able to proceed with the crusade!'

She sat back and gave a deep sigh. Then it dawned on her. 'Oh, yes,' she thought, I took a photo of it on my phone when someone called him out of the office for a couple of minutes. He said I should read it over to make sure I was happy with it. There was only one space for a signature, and I'm sure that's all I need.' She pulled out her phone and swiped through the photos and sure enough it was there, able to be sent to her computer to be printed out.

'Thank you, Holy Spirit for the inspired thought of taking a photo. Who knows what they do in those council offices! They said they would send it to me and they haven't. Takes a woman to get things done around here!' she thought. As relief flooded Linda, so did faith and that faith was released out into the night.

***

Layla stood in the middle of the multitude. Then, as if God had pushed her from behind, she took a step forward. The demon growled angrily. She could feel all the beings around her staring.

'Perhaps if I don't look at my foe,' Layla thought to herself, 'it could be taken as a sign of strength. I don't have the time for this anyway. I've got an assignment and if I have to fight, I will!' She began to walk again. As she advanced, she encountered no opposition. Layla could still feel eyes staring at her, but after a few more steps angels and demons slowly began to turn away, back to what they had been doing before the incident.

Layla continued to walk and passed under the archway, her heart still pounding. She could see no sign of her friends, but saw the stairs and headed for them.

As she reached the foot of the stairs she heard the voice of Trillion for the first time since entering the palace, "I can't hold us much longer.

Quick, up the stairs."

Already the cloak felt lighter. She couldn't see the others anywhere. She bounded up the stairs hoping to find a safe corner to tuck herself away. Her veil flickered. Two other angels were walking down the stairs discussing a matter between themselves as Layla and Trillion ran past them up the stairs. They looked up and saw her. Layla knew that she was now fully exposed, so she purposefully turned and looked into their eyes, hoping they would read her. Both angels nodded and turned from walking down the stairs to follow her with their swords drawn. Layla was no longer cloaked, but she now had Trillion plus the other two angels to help protect her.

"Quick," called Trillion. "We need to get as high as we can before we are stopped." They ran up two and three stairs at a time. The stairway curved around to the left. As they came around the corner, they met Trinity and Samantha who were now also uncloaked. They looked like strong warriors, just as she did.

As Layla met them, Shar and Seraph who were out in front called back to the girls, "Halt!"

The two angels up ahead were wielding swords in each hand, barring the way of five demons who were coming down the stairs. Behind the girls, Trillion and the other two angels were also blocking the way of a dozen demons who were now racing up the stairs in pursuit of the humans. The girls found themselves caught in the middle with nowhere to go.

"We are going to need help," called Trillion. A demon from below drew out an axe with jagged edges and jumped up the stairs towards the defending angels. Trillion leaped into the air and spun with out-stretched arms, clutching a sword in each hand. The first blade sliced through the air in a wide arc with the tip barely missing the demon who had attempted the attack, but in quick succession, the second blade swung around and decapitated his opponent.

"Wait!" shouted another demon, "reinforcements will come, and then we will take them all out!"

Unable to move up or down the girls were forced to play 'the waiting game,' poised in attack positions, with their defenders either side.

***

Linda was in the midst of writing her last email of the evening to the Stadium Convener about the seating arrangements when a picture of Layla floated across the screen of her mind. Linda pushed the thought aside, wanting to get the email finished so that she could go home. It had been a long day. She had begun at 7.00am that morning and had only taken a 20-minute break in the middle of the day for lunch. Linda was getting a little flustered; there were so many elements to consider and organise to run a crusade of this scale. She had learned that nothing in an event 'just' happens. Every detail has to have her attention, or that aspect won't be ready when the time comes. As Linda continued to write, Layla's image came to her mind again, coupled by a prompting to pray. Linda, finding that she was now losing concentration glanced over at her Bible which lay open on her desk. On the right-hand side of the left page about half way down, was a verse that she had highlighted in orange at about the same time last year.

It read, 'And pray in the Spirit on all occasions with all kinds of prayers and requests. With this in mind, be alert and always keep on praying for all the Lord's people.' Ephesians 6:18

These prompts weren't new to Linda; the Lord often asked her to pray for specific things at various times.

"Fine!" she said out loud. She removed her glasses, rubbed her eyes and rested her head on her hands. "Lord, I pray for Layla right now, that you would bless her, and that you would help her with whatever she is in need of right now."

It was a short prayer, but prayed with sincerity and prayed with faith. That was enough. Her prayer set off a chain reaction in the spirit realm. Linda went back to typing her email and finished it within five minutes. She logged out and tipped the rest of her glass of water into the pot of her Marble Queen Pothos plant on her desk. Linda flicked off the light switch, set the alarm, closed the door and locked it. She walked across the carpark feeling satisfied with her day. Her headlights were the last to leave the carpark and drive out of the gates.

***

The prayer she had prayed had risen from her in the form of a glowing orb. The orb was the package containing the substance of her prayer. Her angel was waiting to receive the prayer above her. The spherical prayer container floated into the angel's hands. The angel inspected the orb and saw that it was enough to work with, given the urgency of the situation.

Some prayers are not designed to get used immediately. Prayers are often collected with others until they reach critical mass and then are released. When answers like these are released, there is momentum behind them that brings more breakthroughs that are similar in nature. The cycle of faith releasing answers and answers releasing more faith, generates an environment that wins many battles.

Linda had prayed a prayer purposed for immediate dispatch. The angel quickly slipped the orb into a small satchel slung over his shoulder. Wasting no time, he flew up into the night sky and glided into a slip-stream that immediately sent him hurtling towards Grace Falls. He arrived almost instantly. There was no time for eloquent entrances. He flew into the palace and over the heads of the crowded foyer, under the archway and into the hall. The angel alighted at the base of the stairway and began to run up the stairs. As he ascended, he reached his right hand into a fold in his robes and produced a small silver hammer. With his other hand, he drew out the orb. Up ahead he saw the backs of the demons.

Trillion saw him coming, saw the prayer container and the hammer and said in a commanding voice, "Get ready girls – follow my lead!"

25

TUNNEL
- MISSION LIBERTY -

Liberty continued her journey. After some time her locator indicated that the tunnel she was walking through widened. Up ahead it looked lighter. She neared the place where it opened out. Edging forward slowly, she hoped that she wouldn't see another enemy. Up ahead there was movement. She could hear the eerie echoes of pouring water, the flapping of wings and chattering voices. Liberty pressed her back against the wall ensuring that the shadows were concealing her. Slowly edging along the wall, her surroundings grew lighter. Liberty's forward shoulder felt an alcove, recessed into the wall, as she neared the opening. She slid into the recess and nestled herself into a position giving her a good vantage point from which she could survey what was beyond the opening.

She found herself at the entrance of a large vault. She was about fifteen feet from a watery surface below. The ceiling above was about the same distance from her. Her entrance wasn't the only one. There were five or six other circular tunnel openings into the vault like the one she was standing in. They were half way up the walls between the water and the ceiling. There were also other smaller drains lower down with water pouring out. It was impossible to see how deep the water was because it looked so dark and murky. A few feet below her was a drain that also poured water into the chamber. Around the perimeter of the vault was a ledge that acted as a walkway all the way around to the other side. She might have considered this walkway as the path to take, had the chamber been quiet and empty. But this was not the case at all.

Apart from the structure of the chamber itself, it was the activity within the midst of it that arrested her attention. There were dozens of enemies flying and swooping. Some perched on the ledge and others found clefts in the roof from which to hang. They all seemed to maintain their altitude, not getting too close to the surface of the water below. She saw two demons enter the room via one of the drain openings. One of them passed a package to another, who then took it and flew off. The demon who had taken the bundle was escorted by another and disappeared into one of the other tunnels on the other side of the chamber.

'Looks like a gathering point, a place where exchanges happen. I wonder what the packages are?' she thought.

Another demon entered the vault holding a package loosely bundled in cloth and started to circle the room, 'Perhaps in a holding pattern until its off-load arrives,' she thought.

As it circled close, above the background chatter of noise, she heard the demon mumbling to itself, "Keys, keys, it is always keys…" Its voice trailed off as it swooped around the room again.

It drew near and continued to mumble, "More to give, more to try…" Just then another demon entered and looked around the room, searching for its contact. The demon holding the package flew towards it, thrust the bundle into the receiver's chest and disappeared out of the chamber without so much as another word. The remaining demon inspected its acquisition, grunted, then disappeared up another drain.

"Keys!" Liberty said. "Are they searching for the keys to the city? Has the enemy lost them?" directing her question to no-one in particular.

Just then a waft of stale air blew past her, accompanied by a demon, who was using very the tunnel that she had been travelling through. She pressed herself further into the alcove. It flew past, unaware of her presence.

'God, is there another way? I'm never going to get to the other side of this chamber unseen.' As she was about to retreat, she smelled the same stale air and pressed herself against the wall. Another demon flew past just as the previous one had.

'God, I'm stuck now. What do I do?' No answer came. Knowing that she couldn't stay there forever, she looked out again for possible ways that she could get through.

As she looked out, her gaze was drawn down towards the water. She noticed a light patch in the middle of the water. Liberty hadn't noticed it before. As she strained to see what it was, she saw that it extended from right beneath her to the far end of the chamber in a straight line. 'A submerged walkway? Even if it is a walkway, it doesn't help me. No way am I walking out in full view of all these demons,' she thought. 'I wonder why the demons are staying high.'

As she looked along the walkway, her vision sharpened so that she was able to see more clearly. Liberty was intrigued by what she saw.

Her lift in clarity revealed that, rather than a walkway, she was looking at a faint tube of light, like a tunnel, running along the surface of the water. She didn't know why she hadn't noticed it before, but it was quite evident now. Maybe her vision and understanding were heightening to see more detail of the spiritual realm in which she found herself. Liberty was in a situation that was forcing her to look deeper. There didn't seem to be any other way. The tube looked more and more like a tunnel. Just then, she saw a flash of light shoot through it. She focused again, another flash of light shot through the tunnel. As she looked intently, focusing on the next flash, time slowed down, waiting for her to catch up. But it wasn't just a flash; she saw wings and the outline of a figure. As it got a little further away, time sped up again, and it shot off into the distance.

'This place is an interchange,' she thought, 'A place where demons make exchanges as they pass through and angels also glide through towards their destination, unnoticed by those hovering above. Demons swoop in, while angels shoot past.'

The demons didn't seem to notice the flashes. 'I wonder why they can't see it? I wonder if they even know that it is there? If I got down to the tunnel, could I travel through it myself undetected?'

As she considered this, she remembered the portion of scripture from Isaiah 55:12, 'be led forth in peace.' That was it. She did feel at peace when she considered the idea.

'How do I get down there? I can't just miraculously drop five metres down. I can't lower myself down, it would take too long, and they would see me.'

Just then another demon glided past her and into the chamber, but it didn't go too far before it arced back around and alighted on the edge of her tunnel, very close to where she was hiding. Its claws gripped the edge of the ledge. Its head cocked to one side as if listening to something. It then turned its head and slowly to look straight in her direction. It didn't seem like the demon knew what it was looking at because the shadow was still dark enough to conceal Liberty. It advanced towards her, peering into the darkness, with its beady little eyes, slowly rocking its head from side to side.

'Can it sense me?' Previously Liberty may have panicked, but now, having encountered a lot of demons over the last few hours, and also killing some, she found that her whole body was calm. She could almost feel its breath on her face. She slowly reached her left hand down to take hold of her sword strapped to her right thigh and gently drew it out of its sheath. Her intention was to slash the demon back into the tunnel so that she didn't draw attention to herself. Her arm tensed, then with all her might she thrust the blade across her body and sliced upwards through the demon with ease.

Unfortunately, the top half of the demon fell out into the opening and splashed into the water below.

'Move now!' she heard the Holy Spirit say, as she rushed to the edge in full view, looked down and noticed a single pipe protruding from the wall just below her. She immediately sheathed her sword, spun with her back to the room and dropped onto the pipe below. The commotion behind her sent shivers up her spine. She spun around again and jumped from the pipe and landed within the tunnel of light, facing her enemies.

But as her feet touched the base of the tube they suddenly slid out from under her, and she fell backward, landing softly on her back. Immediately her whole body shot forward. Time slowed for a moment as she focused on what was above her. She saw the demons hovering in slow motion. They were looking in her general direction but did not seem to focus their gaze directly upon her. 'They can no longer see me,' she thought. Then suddenly time returned, and the room was gone. She felt herself rapidly shooting through tunnels and vaults and chambers.

She had discovered a slip stream that angels use to travel between points, like angel highways. Start points and intersections of the pathways are places where the kingdom of God has dominion. These are usually churches or places where people encounter God frequently. The moment she had dropped into the tunnel of light, she became completely immersed within it, invisible to the enemy. In that one moment, she was gone and found herself transported to another part of the city.

The speed took her breath away.

"Lord…" was all she could say as she was locked into a lying down position, with her hands at her sides. She was still on her first gasp of air. It was like being in shock, shooting down an unexpectedly fast hydro-slide. She forced her lungs to exhale and breathed in again in an attempt to gain control of her respiratory system. She found that her mind was able to catch up after a few seconds could process the high speeds. The rooms seemed to shoot past less quickly as her consciousness heightened. She continued on her journey to an unknown destination.

Then, as if prompted, she remembered her locator. Liberty lifted her arm to see where her target was. By this time, she had gone a long way past where the keys were, and Liberty was now rapidly moving out of the city. Up ahead it looked like the stream split into two. In a split second, she elected to go right and rolled her body in that direction. She blasted into the tube of light on the right and was launched upwards faster than she had ever travelled before. She shot through layers of rock and stone and then erupted out of the ground, up into the air. Her eyes grew wide, gathering as much information as possible.

As she travelled unbelievably fast, Liberty looked around and noticed other streams that looked like ribbons of light stretched across the sky. She scanned for one that would take her back down to where she wanted to go before she ended up in another hemisphere. There was a stream coming up fast on her left that intersected hers. She leaned hard left and managed the transition. Like lightning, she shot back down, through the atmosphere and plunged underground towards her goal. Her locator indicated that she was getting close.

She passed through a large room that looked empty and immediately rolled completely out of the stream. The forces on her body suddenly slackened off, and she was sent skidding across the floor. She spread out her arms and legs to slow herself. Liberty pressed down hard with her heels and hands on to the gravelly concrete in an attempt to stop the slide, managing to reduce her speed and gently hit the wall at the far end of the room.

Liberty sat up breathing hard, senses still heightened after her experience. She looked around, her mind buzzing from the ride. Her pulse was still racing as she found herself in 'fight or flight' mode. Her eyes flashed around the room, was she alone here? The room was empty. Liberty relaxed her concentration and started to giggle as a stress relief.

"What was that?! I've just had the ride of my life." She chuckled, "That was too awesome!"

She sat for a while in the darkened room with her legs straight out in front of her, leaning back on her hands. Still smiling and then shaking her head, she thought, 'Roller-coasters are going to feel very tame after that.' Liberty let out a deep sigh, "God, I need a break." There was no response. She knew she had to get up and so spent time refocusing, mentally preparing herself to move on.

Her locator pointed her in the direction of some tunnels up ahead. As she neared them, she couldn't figure out which of the three to take. Her locator pointed in their general direction. She chose the central one because it was the largest of the three and it felt more 'right' than the others.

Liberty came to a point where the tunnel stopped and opened out into another chamber. She felt a breeze and looked up. There were metal grates above her on road-level that allowed dim light to enter and stripe the wall with shadows. Across the room was a huge round door with a wheel in the middle of it, that looked like it would open the door if she could get it to turn.

Liberty was about to step out into the light, but then suddenly darted back into the shadow. She had just noticed two figures, one on each side of the door, sitting almost motionless, as if sleeping. They were shrouded in cloaks, but she could also see the glistening point of a spear protruding from each. They were guards. 'How will I get past these two?' she pondered.

26

ELEMENTAL STONE
- mission boys -

"I can just see it!" About 100 paces away was the Elemental Stone. Caden couldn't see it clearly because there were a lot of demons milling around obstructing his view. Both on the ground and also in the air, many demons were gathering within the vicinity of the sacred object.

Just then, a gap opened up in the crowd, and Caden caught his first real glimpse. The Elemental Stone was mesmerising. It looked like a giant ruby set in a golden clasp. The stone was a little taller than Caden himself and red in colour. It looked alive. A swirling liquid was furiously spinning within it. There was a rapid shifting of light and dark patches. The dark areas seemed to be the evidence of the enemy's control, firstly spinning in one direction and then fiercely changing to another. It appeared that the substance within the stone was fighting to break out. It behaved like a whirlpool of energy spinning within its heart. Any standard particles would have been torn apart with the sudden altering of direction at that speed. Elements raged within the stone.

The clasp looked to have grown out of the ground, and its golden branch-like arms wrapped themselves around the bottom half of the Elemental Stone, fixing it firmly to the clifftop.

"It's amazing," exclaimed Caden in awe. "You gotta see this."

Tristan positioned himself to get a look at it. Side by side, they peered from their vantage point and found themselves transfixed by its appearance. As they gazed deeper into the stone, they could see eyes, many eyes. 'These are the eyes of wisdom,' thought Tristan to himself.

"It's alive," he said. "It's a living being like one of the four living creatures with eyes all over, which surround the throne of God in the book of Revelation."

"We need to set it free," said Caden. "But now that we are here, I don't even know what we are supposed to do and how to do it! What do you reckon?"

"Yeah, we will get nowhere near it with so many demons around. We will barely be able to take a few steps without being seen."

There was a silence between them as they settled back down into their shelter. The shelter was simply a ledge, nestled under an overhang, but it gave the boys the cover that they needed. From there, Caden and Tristan could see all of Riverdale, set against the backdrop of a starry night. Tristan closed his eyes.

After some time he said, "We need God to speak to us and show us what to do." He paused thoughtfully, "What is the first verse from the Bible that comes to your mind?"

Caden thought and said, "The first one for me is: 'For where two or three gather in my name, there am I with them.'"

"Good start," said Tristan. "I was thinking of that one too. There were three of us, but now, even with two, like the verse says, I'm sure we can do whatever we need to do. Another verse comes to mind in Luke which says: 'At sunset, the people brought to Jesus all who had various kinds of sickness, and laying his hands on each one, he healed them.' I get the feeling that we just need to put our hands on the stone. Maybe that is enough."

"Yep, sounds good to me. With no other leads at this stage, I'm happy for that to be the goal. But we are only going to get one shot at this. There is a host of demons between us and the stone. We need a plan!" Caden said.

"Yep," agreed Tristan. "We can't just make a run for it. It's too far for that. We need a diversion."

"One of us could create a diversion, while the other makes a run for it," suggested Caden.

"We could, but I feel like we both have to lay our hands on the Elemental Stone together."

Caden and Tristan sat, praying and thinking. 'We need a strategy, but we also need to understand timing too because time is running out,' pondered Tristan. 'The right action at the wrong time could mean disaster, just as doing the wrong thing at the right time could also mean total failure. It isn't just about us either because the other two teams are also relying on us. Even if they succeed, if we can't get to the Elemental Stone we all fail. God help us to know your strategy.' Tristan's thoughts continued to tumble through his mind, 'Our actions will either cut off or maintain the life-blood of our city. The golden thread of hope that has weaved through the streets since its conception must not be severed by us, through misinterpreted signs and misguided activity.' Lightning struck again.

'God show us what we need to do.' Caden's thoughts drifted, 'I wonder how the others are doing. Oh yes, I need to pray.' Liberty came to mind. 'Lord I pray that you would help Liberty. Protect her. Help her to fulfil her task. Give her victory!'

Just as he said the word 'victory,' he saw a mist rise from around him. The prayer haze was white and radiated from his head and shoulders. He saw it climb into the sky, disperse, and then fade into the night.

27

windows
- mission girls -

The angel stopped five steps away from the demons that were closest to him. They all spun around and saw the familiar sight of an orb.

"No!" shouted a demon. "Don't let him release it!" Unaffected by the demon protest, the angel held the prayer container in front of him and raised the hammer, poised to strike. Suddenly the hammer was shot from his grasp, hit by a dagger that a demon had thrown who rushed in from behind. The hammer was flung through the air and clanged against the wall, then clattered down the steps only to be picked up by another demon who was rapidly advancing up the stairs.

Trinity flicked her eyes from the angel with the orb to look at Trillion, hoping to gain some comfort, expecting to see a confident expression, but his expression was stern and grave. Quickly glancing around looking for a sign of hope, she remembered a verse from Daniel, '… the prince of the Persian kingdom resisted me twenty-one days. Then Michael, one of the chief princes, came to help me because I was detained there with the king of Persia.'

'I'm actually here,' she thought, 'Caught in the crossfire of angelic warfare. This is epic!'

It was all on now. The entire palace was on alert. The cloaking had got them half way, but now the situation required an abrupt change in strategy. They braced themselves for battle.

Layla, aware that more demons were advancing, thought to herself, 'What can I do? If I'm going to do something, I need to do it fast.'

The orb and the hammer seemed to be of prime importance, though she didn't know what they would do. 'Perhaps they are a weapon of some sort,' she thought. 'God I need your help!' Instantly a bow materialised in her hand with an arrow in the other. Even though she had never used a bow and arrow on the surface, she was a skilled marksman in this realm. Acting fast, she loaded the arrow and drew the string back in an instant. Layla aimed the point of the arrow at the demon who had picked up the hammer, and she released it into the air. It sailed straight through the demon, and out the other side. The arrow continued its trajectory and proceeded into another demon that was advancing up the stairs.

Seraph seized the moment as Layla loaded a second arrow that had appeared in her hand. Drawing both of his swords Seraph jumped down the steps and sliced through a demon on each side of him. The one who had picked up the hammer now lay crumpled on the floor. Seraph stood over the beast and took possession of the hammer. Making eye contact with the angel who was still holding the orb, Seraph threw the hammer to him. The angel raised his hand, caught it, and in one movement brought it down onto the prayer package shattering it like glass. Its substance was released instantaneously like the air from a balloon when popped. The smoky substance dispersed like an explosion. The majority of it shot sideways, blowing a hole in the wall, large enough for the girls to escape. The rest of the prayer dispersed up and down the stairs, knocking the demons in the vicinity to the ground unconscious.

"That's your path," shouted Trillion as he pointed towards the hole that had been smashed through the wall. "Go!" Layla slung the bow over her back and jumped through the opening. Samantha and Trinity followed close behind. The angels did not follow. Some guarded the entrance while Shar, Seraph, and Trillion raced up the stairs towards the great courtyard where they knew the girls would need to cross if they were to get to the throne.

The girls burst out of the opening and found themselves halfway up the cliff face of Grace Falls. It was a long way down. The river looked much smaller from their new vantage point. They had stepped out on to a terrace which was cantilevered out from the cliff. The girls raced along its gentle upward slope, following the contours of the cliff face. Up ahead Samantha saw that it continued under the waterfall. The girls made for the falls, hoping that the cascading water would help to conceal them from view. Samantha didn't like being exposed on the face for all to see.

The falls arched over the terrace, creating a tunnel of water and mist. As they entered the tunnel, the spray of the falls refreshed their faces. It was exhilarating having thousands of litres of water pouring over their heads. It was like being a surfer caught in the tube of a twenty-foot wave. The cascading water made a thunderous sound that filled the misty air around them. As they quickly progressed along the terrace under the falls, Layla started to get a little dizzy as she looked at the water rapidly descending to the river below. By this time, the sound of the water was almost deafening. The all-consuming roaring sound, coupled with a perpetually moving wall of thousands of litres of water was enough to make all of them struggle to maintain their focus.

As they came out from under the waterfall, they started to pass a series of windows chiselled into the cliff face. These arch-shaped windows led to various rooms within the mountainside of Grace Falls.

Trinity who was now out in front called back, "We should choose one of these rooms to go into, rather than being exposed like this. They will spot us out here in no time."

"Should we just choose a window at random? At least it should buy us some time so that we can figure out which is the best way to the throne."

Each window had a frame of individually and uniquely crafted carvings. As they passed more and more windows, they noticed letters and numbers carved into the sills of each.

"Hey, these are Bible references," called out Layla.

"Do you see any that you recognise?" Samantha shouted back.

Layla looked closer and recognised one. "Matt 11:28, I have just read this recently, I think it is about, 'rest for the weary.'"

"Sounds good, but is it going to help us?"

They continued to pass more and more windows.

"2 Tim 3:17, is being equipped for every good work."

"Could be good, but I feel like we already have the equipping that we need." Samantha then added, "We can't just guess which window to go in, we need to have a reason. Faith always has a reason; it always has a purpose. We are on a quest and are advancing against an enemy that wants to kill us and destroy our city."

"You are right," said Layla, "we can't drop our guard, we need to be smart and need to choose wisely."

"This is it!" shouted Trinity. "I know this one. It's one of my favourite verses, Isaiah 40:31 '…soar on wings like eagles.' We need to get high, and if we can get a lift from an eagle, we could get to the throne in no time."

Layla and Samantha came up to the window that Trinity was looking at. The three girls looked at each other breathing hard, then peered through the window into a dimly lit room.

"Yes!" said Samantha. "I don't think there is any point going on and trying to find a window that seems more 'right.' I feel that if we pass this one up, there may not be a chance of getting back to it, even if we wanted to. I wonder if we can take this verse literally. Anyway, we've been out here long enough. Do we all agree?" Each nodded.

"Then let's go in," said Trinity. Just as Trinity was about to hoist herself up onto the ledge, Samantha spotted a demon perched on a rocky outcrop a few yards away, staring at them angrily.

"Demon!" alerted Samantha as she pointed toward the creature.

As quick as a flash Layla drew out her bow, loaded it, aimed and released the string, all within moments. The arrow shot from the bow and pierced the demon through the chest.

"Didn't see that coming did he?!" said Layla in an aggressive tone.

"Ouch! Wouldn't want to be your enemy!" said Trinity with a surprised look on her face, becoming more and more impressed by the confidence and skill that her friends were displaying. The three girls had begun to notice how quickly they had been growing in faith, demonstrating the qualities you would expect of daughters of a great king. It was an awakening within, a transition from girlhood to womanhood, a transition from being led, to being entrusted with the responsibility of governing themselves, and eventually an entire realm.

"Okay girls, we need to focus. You ready to go in?" asked Layla. The other two nodded.

"Then let's go!"

28

EAGLES
- mission girls -

Layla was the first to climb onto the window sill. The room was cool and smelt of sweet rosewood. She dropped down over the other side of the ledge and onto a wooden panelled floor. The other two followed. The panelling over the floor was stepped out in a diagonal pattern that covered the entire surface. In the middle of the floor was a large rectangular Persian-style rug. Various intricate patterns of purple, crimson, gold and sapphire blue tessellated across it. The girls looked around wide-eyed, unsure of what they should be looking for or what they would find. The room seemed empty apart from the rug in the middle of the floor and carved wooden statues of eagles stationed around the edges of the chamber. The eagles were about ten feet high with their heads almost reaching the ceiling. With wings folded in and heads held high, the gaze of each was set in towards the centre of the room.

"Not much happening in this room," said Trinity

"No, apart from these freaky statues, there doesn't seem to be anything else here," said Layla.

"Yeah, a little freaky, but they also look so majestic and powerful. They could be guardians," said Samantha, who loved admiring the evidence of God's creation.

"We need to keep moving," Layla said, looking for an exit.

The girls proceeded towards a door on the opposite side of the room. As they crossed onto the rug, they heard breath released from behind them and felt it blow through their hair. All three spun around in fright to see one of the eagles coming to life and ruffling its feathers. Having been awakened from an age-long sleep, it stretched out its enormous wings, then settled itself and stared at the three with its eagle eyes. With no offered expression, it locked its gaze onto the three girls and blinked. There was no escape from this powerful creature. Portions of scripture flashed into Layla's mind. She thought of the places in the Bible that spoke of eagles such as Psalm 103, Ezekiel, Revelation, and others. The mention of eagles in these places of the Bible portrayed them in a favourable and helpful disposition to the purposes of God.

Trinity was the first to speak, "Will you help us?"

The eagle blinked again and continued to stare at the three. Suddenly it stepped out from its place against the wall, startling the girls. It took a couple of steps closer, then opened its beak and breathed over them. It had happened so quickly that they all just stood motionless for a moment. The breath from the beast felt warm and energising. Layla felt a tingling sensation all over her body.

'What is happening to me? I feel like I'm wearing waves of energy, kinda like those shimmering heatwaves that rise off the asphalt when you're looking at a road on a hot day. But it's all around me,' thought Trinity.

The feeling intensified and seemed to soak into her skin.

'Something is happening to me. I feel like I'm in a cocoon, wrapped in brilliant liquid light, about to be re-birthed into something majestic,' thought Samantha in wonder.

The girls were lifted into the air a little, drawn up with the breath of the eagle. Trinity closed her eyes, took a deep breath and felt a small explosion come from within her chest like a burst of power as she landed gently on the ground. The burst of energy felt like it had blasted away the cocoon from around her. Her old clothing and skin were discarded, revealing new life underneath.

The dreamy state of the experience contrasted sharply with the drop to the ground and left her wondering, 'How did I fall so gracefully?' Her newly inherited wings had splayed out to cushion the landing. She looked across the room, Layla and Samantha were getting their wings too.

"I have wings?!" Trinity said to herself in amazement. "How sweet is this!"

The three stared at each other with huge smiles.

Just then the door burst open. The girls spun to face the door. Swords materialised in Trinity and Samantha's hands, and Layla had her bow at the ready. They had lost all sense of time being caught up in their experience. A wave of relief flooded them when the saw Shar, Seraph and Trillion hurry into the room.

"How did you find us?" asked Layla.

"I've been assigned to you, Layla, I always know where you are," replied Shar. "This is the advantage that we have. Now I also see that you have another advantage too," as he motioned towards Layla's wings. We can no longer go on foot anyway; the enemy has set roadblocks in various places. But we now have the element of surprise as they will not suspect that you have wings. It will now be an all-out race to the throne. We must be swift."

The six of them turned and exited the room through the window that the girls had entered. They stepped back out into the open, back on to the path, high up the cliff face.

"Now," said Shar. "We don't have much time. You will be safer in the air than standing on this ledge, but you will need to have faith, especially for your initial jump. Faith will keep you in the air, just as faith kept Peter walking on water. These wings will take you where you want to go as long as you maintain your confidence in God during flight."

"Don't worry," Shar assured them. "The longer you are airborne, the easier it gets… just don't over-think it," Shar added. He had been growing very fond of his human companions. He was also confident in their abilities. God had chosen them for this mission after all.

"I'm ready," said Trinity. "Ready to take a leap of faith. Let's finish this!" The others nodded.

Trinity set her gaze resolutely to the horizon, 'I'm not waiting! Got to do this now, before I over think this and get freaked out.'

With that, she ran and jumped with arms stretched out in front of her. As an extension of her body and spirit, her wings spread wide. All fears and reservations remained on the solid ground behind her. The wind tossed her hair backward as she embraced the open expanse.

"It's incredible!" Trinity yelled. Testing her control, she lifted her left arm a little and lowered her right arm; her wings followed and arced her back around toward the cliff. Samantha took courage and also jumped with her arms spread wide. As she drew her hands to her sides, her wings followed suit, resulting in a graceful dive. Feeling exhilarated, she spread her arms to catch an updraft and rose again, level with the others. Layla, who was enjoying watching her friends and just about to jump, turned and smiled at Shar. Just then an arrow struck the ground beside her startling her, then another to the left and before she could leap, a third pierced her wing, causing it to crumble away and turn to dust.

"Go!" Shar shouted at Seraph and Trillion. "Get the other two girls to the throne!" The angels launched into the air to join Trinity and Samantha.

"We must go now," Seraph called to the girls. "Our mission depends on it. Shar will look after Layla."

The four flew away from the cliff, out of range of the arrows. Demons peeled off the cliff in pursuit.

"We must get high," called Seraph. "We can out-fly them. Speed is on our side."

The girls focused their attention on gaining altitude and found that they had impressive speed. They left the trailing demons in the dust, yelling and cursing. A few arrows were shot in a vain attempt, only to fall short and plummet toward the ground far below, much to the demons' dismay.

Seraph and Trillion flew on, with the girls in between them. They continued to climb, clearing the top of the cliff. The scene that met their eyes was awesome and horrifying. There below them was a large plain occupied by the enemy. Hundreds, if not thousands of demons populated it, standing in military formations. The land had crisscrossed walkways dividing the troops indicating divisions and ranks. Some units appeared motionless, while others were engaged in a lot more movement. At various places on the plain, the ordered patterns were disrupted and scattered outwards.

"Demons are not very good at holding formation," called Trillion. "They fight and snap at each other. Most of them haven't seen us yet, and most of them won't see us until it is too late because they get so consumed by their offences and arguments."

The demons' preoccupation comforted Samantha. They had the element of surprise and also had Shar and Trillion at their side helping them. What could go wrong?

"God, look after Layla," Samantha prayed. "Protect her and show her what to do."

Then, as if prompted, Samantha said, "Lord, give the boys success. We are now down to the wire. Hook them up with what they need."

As she said this, a stream of silver ejected from each of her hands. The streams shot ahead of her, intertwining into a single cord that disappeared into the distance in the direction of Razor Peak.

29

STRIKE

- mission boys -

Caden sat staring out over the landscape, thinking.

Tristan was the first to speak, "Hey remember what the angel said at our commissioning. He said when the time comes you would know that to do."

"Yeah, I was thinking about that too. But, to be honest, I don't know what to do."

Just then, the boys heard voices above them getting closer to the edge. One of the demons coughed and spluttered, "Arggg, I hate this cough, what are you looking at?!"

"Oh shut up, I'm in charge of this assignment, you're just here to back me up."

"Yeah, whatever, just keep looking."

'What are they looking for?' thought Caden, 'I hope not us. We've got no chance if they know we are coming.'

Just then, lightning struck a metal structure on the top of a building situated on the edge of Central Park, downtown. The crack reverberated around the surrounding mountains, and the flash left a bright spot in Caden's vision for a few seconds.

"Ha, close enough!" called the demon. "Not long now. Let's go report it."

Arguing between the demons started up again as their voices trailed off into the distance.

The bright spot in Caden's vision was fading.

He waited a few more seconds until it was quiet above and then whispered to Tristan, "Okay, that helps. I've noticed that the lightning strikes are becoming more frequent, yet the cloud cover seems to have been constant throughout our time here. It's not getting stormier."

"The strikes have been getting closer to us too," Tristan responded.

"So, the strikes must be a part of the answer because we know that the Elemental Stone and the atmosphere of the city are linked."

"If they've been getting closer and more frequent, it must be some sort of countdown. Remember how the angel talked about the atmosphere setting a clock. It makes sense that if the strikes are getting closer and more frequent, that a countdown could be culminated by a final strike, perhaps on the Elemental Stone itself. If that is the case, we must finish our assignment before that last strike," said Tristan

"Okay, well, if it is a countdown, like an atmospheric clock, then we should be able to work out a pattern as to when a strike will happen next," suggested Caden.

"Great thought. How about this..." said Tristan, thinking out loud. "Perhaps we can time it so that we make our move when we get a really close strike. The blinding light may help to conceal us, gaining us an extra couple of seconds to make the dash for it. Might be wishful thinking though." Tristan paused as another idea emerged in his mind, "Or what if we could even harness a strike." He followed the new train of thought. Tristan didn't realise, but his thought processes were beginning to be led by the Holy Spirit. He was gaining the mind of Christ for the task at hand.

"If we had some wire, we could tie a strand of wire to one of your arrows and use your crossbow to shoot it over the enemy horde. It would need to land behind them so that the length of wire falls right through the masses. We could then take the other end of the wire and attach it to another arrow to shoot into the sky. If the lightning struck the skyward arrow, the lightning would trace through the wire and be conducted right through the middle of the enemy."

"Wow! That could work. We just need some wire, good timing, and a great shot," said Caden.

"Let's just pray for some wire. If it comes, then it would help to confirm that the plan may actually work."

Just then lightning struck even closer. Tristan quickly commenced his stopwatch. 'Time runs differently here,' he thought. He remembered the angel talked about time in this realm taking less than on the surface."

"Let's pray! Lord Jesus, your word says that you will supply all of our needs. Please now provide us with wire that we can use to create a diversion to help us get to the stone and complete our mission."

Just then, Trinity's prayer arrived, a silver thread in the sky, flying towards them from the north-east, the direction of Grace Falls. In no time, the silver streak was suddenly in front of them. The boys jumped out of the way so as not to be hit. It hit the ledge between them, and then the thread traced a circle on the ground, creating a coil. As the length of thread came to an end, the boys found themselves looking at the very thing for which they had prayed. Caden picked it up. It was metallic like wire but very soft and flexible like string.

"I like it!" said Caden.

Lightning struck again, and Tristan glanced down at his watch,

"That is eight minutes exactly since the last strike."

Caden took an end of the wire and started to work on the arrows. He selected two arrows and tied the wire to the feather end of the first, and then with the other end of the wire did the same to the second. Caden took the time to make sure that his knots were secure and that they wouldn't get tangled in the mechanics of the crossbow when he fired them. Another strike.

Tristan looked at his watch, "That strike hit exactly four minutes since the previous hit. If the period between strikes halves each time, we have less than two minutes to make this happen. We are very close to the end. It is now or never."

Above them, they could hear the increasing cacophony of noise from the enemy increasing, shouts, screeches, metal on metal, and the ground trembling with many footsteps. Feeling the tension building, Caden loaded his bow with the first arrow and peered over the ledge again. He could see the enemy becoming increasingly restless, pounding each other on the chest and knocking shields together, hyping themselves up for a fight. He lifted the arrow into place, raised the crossbow, breathed in deeply, focusing on a target beyond the army of demons, exhaled and pulled the trigger. The arrow whistled high over the crowd and disappeared unnoticed on the other side, somewhere behind the chaotic enemy masses. The arc of wire, created by the trajectory of the arrow, started to fall to the ground and alight on the enemy below. Caden loaded the other arrow while Tristan commenced a countdown from 15 seconds.

"I'll shoot at 3 seconds to give the arrow time to fly; then we need to jump."

"6, 5, 4, 3..."

The arrow launched into the air, but as Caden released it, he felt the string twang back in an awkward direction.

"Oh no!" cried Caden. The arrow had half the power behind it that Caden had anticipated. The misfire caused it to shoot out at an angle instead of straight up, way too close to the cliff and nowhere near the highest point in the vicinity. The shot signalled 'mission over.' Caden and Tristan helplessly watched as the arrow curved over on its descent toward the ground, taking their wire with it. The boys felt sick and sensed the sentence of 'fail' in their hearts.

***

On the surface, Gabriella was immediately alerted. She was a prophet and an intercessor and was out for dinner with her friends. As she sat at the table surrounded by conversation, a picture of an arrow flashed in her mind. The image flashed again. It was such a strong impression that she immediately excused herself from the table, got up, and proceeded towards the toilets, praying under her breath as she walked. Gabriella was one of the particular ones that the Holy Spirit called on when immediate assistance was needed. It wasn't so much that she was more special to God than others, rather, she had learned obedience; therefore God could trust her with the promptings that he released. When God required the human intervention of faith, he often used Gabriella. She would do what he asked immediately.

"Arrow fly," she prayed. "Arrow fly!" There was nothing else that she could pray. All she saw was a golden arrow, back-dropped by a dark sky.

"Arrow fly!" she commanded, and then she blew.

***

Her breath immediately translated into the spirit realm. Caden and Tristan looked out over the edge of the cliff, staring down at the descending arrow. Just then, a blast of air thundered up the cliff face. The massive updraft roared in the ears of the boys, causing them to scrunch their eyes up tightly. They were lifted up and thrown into the back of the ledge that they were on. Stunned, the boys opened their eyes in time to see the arrow hurtle past them, and within a second it was high up above them.

Strike!

There was a deafening crack. Lightning struck the airborne arrow which shattered into tiny blazing fragments. The blinding explosion illuminated the surrounding cloud cover. Electricity shot along the wire that was momentarily suspended in the sky. The blinding electrical energy raced down the wire toward the earth. As the electric current hit the ledge, there was a huge flash where the remainder of the coil was lying. Then there was another flash, as the light traced up the remaining wire and over the ledge. A huge uproar erupted above them.

"Go, go, go!" yelled Caden.

The boys jumped up, flung themselves over the top of the cliff and made a wild dash for the stone.

A wide scorch mark trailed along the ground and into the crowd. It branched off in many directions as the electricity was conducted through weapons and armour. The demons were dropping like flies as the electricity tore through them. There was smoke, fire, bodies lying on the ground, shouting and absolute chaos. Many of the enemy soldiers were rolling around, groaning, holding injured and charred parts of their body. The plan seemed to have worked so far.

The boys had already covered most of the distance to the Elemental Stone before the first of the enemy spotted them. A demon let out a loud roar as it pointed towards the boys, alerting others. The demons' focus shifted, and they launched themselves at the boys, determined to take them out before they reached the stone. Some demons fell as they ran, too badly burnt and injured to continue, others continued to hobble but a couple who had avoided the strike, fully mobile, with fury in their eyes, raced at the boys ready for battle. Just metres from reaching the stone, a demon made it into the path of the pair. Caden raised his crossbow and slammed it down hard on the head of the beast. The impact cracked the helmet it was wearing, and it fell to the ground.

The boys pushed their bodies to move as fast as they could. Tristan felt a surge of adrenaline racing through the muscles of his legs. His steps turned into strides, covering as much ground as possible with every bound. He swung his arms as he ran as if reaching for the stone. The synapses in his brain were firing with such intensity that the whole scene seemed to slow down and he could process all the information that was entering through his eye-gate. He glanced at the closest demon and was amazed that he could pick out the finest detail. Drool from its teeth splayed out into droplets around its ferocious head. The battle-scarred armour that hung from bone and muscle jolted with each stride as the monster furiously rushed nearer. All around were the sounds of shouts, screeches, metal on metal, and the thud of footsteps and bodies slamming into each other.

Out of the corner of his eye he saw an angel locked in combat with two demons, 'That's one from the roof!' he thought, 'They are buying us time.'

The Elemental Stone was almost within reach. Two steps before the stone, the boys looked into each other's dirty faces, wide-eyed, but full of determination. Both boys raised an outstretched arm and slapped a hand onto the stone at the same time. At that moment a ring of amber light shot out from the Elemental Stone, flattening the entire enemy horde. The boys were knocked off their feet and thrown backward. Tristan felt winded as he fell hard to the ground. Caden had the presence of mind to twist his body around to avoid landing flat on his back. He hit the ground on his side and skidded across the gravel. The impact of the amber light erased the enemy from the field of battle.

As the boys opened their eyes and lifted themselves up, they found themselves to be the only ones left on the top of Razor Peak. The ground was littered with bits and pieces of armour and weapons, but no bodies could be seen amongst the debris. With a tremendous feeling of relief, they turned to look at the stone and noticed it change. The dark patches from within were draining out of it and seeping away into the ground.

The internal substance of the stone continued to exude energy and life and the atmosphere around it was changing. Clouds above the Elemental Stone began to part and the sky cleared. The boys looked at each other smiling. Relief flooded over them as the realisation of having achieved their mission dawned on them.

They noticed the clasp that held the Elemental Stone in place was changing colour. It was becoming more like the colour of the stone itself. Then a sudden trail of red rock shot along the ground. It became a glassy pathway of ruby that ran along the surface and over the cliff face. A brilliant trail of red could be seen shooting towards the centre of the city. The bright ribbon continued due east, but skirted around obstacles such as buildings and traced through roads and over grassy reserves. A wall of dazzling red light followed the path across the city like a silk curtain hanging in the sky. The boys had secured the Stone and re-established the red axis.

30

VAULT
- MISSION LIBERTY -

As Liberty sat, she noticed a mist dropping down into the room through the grates in the ceiling above. She edged back and continued to look to see what would happen.

The mist hung in drifts down the walls like smoky fingers reaching to the floor below. As the haze covered the two figures who were guarding the door, the one on the left keeled over and slumped onto the paved stonework. The one on the right jumped up to its feet startled. It took a couple of steps, then fell face first heavily onto the stone. The mist continued to drift down and seep into the floor beneath. Within minutes the mist was gone just as silently as it had come.

'Someone's praying for me!' Liberty recognised the divine intervention on her behalf. The prayer support prompted her to pray for the others.

"I pray for Samantha, Trinity, and Layla. Protect them. Help them to get to the throne and bring them success." As she prayed for the girls, two beams of laser light shot up from either side of her like spinning helicopter blades and vanished into the skies above.

"That's for you," she said with a smile. She was pleased to have seen her prayer take form.

Liberty emerged from her hiding place and stood, surveying the scene before her. The two lifeless figures remained motionless on the floor. A glow from the grates above illuminated the millions of dust particles in the room which danced and flickered in the light. The particles gently swirled about, stirred by the gentle breeze which chilled her face as she looked toward the grates. Liberty stepped over the demon that lay lifelessly face-down in the middle of the floor. Its cloak had disturbed the dusty surface which left evidence of the impact as the creature had hit the ground. Streaks on the floor radiated outwards from the collision. She stepped quickly across the room and stopped at the large door in front of her. Glancing at the ground behind her, she also noticed impressions from the soles of her boots tracing her footsteps through the dust to the door. With both hands, she gripped the wheel at the centre of the door and tried desperately to move it. With the tops of her knuckles whitening, she used all the strength she could muster to generate some movement. Finally, with a cracking sound, like a seal breaking, the wheel reluctantly turned a few degrees. After a short rest, she tried again. It was freer this time, and the door began to slide open. She opened it enough to be able to peer through. There seemed to be no movement inside so she continued to push it open and slipped into the vault. As she stepped into the room, she saw about a dozen demons lying on the floor just like the two outside.

'They must have been knocked out by the same mist. God, you know how long I need to be here. Please don't let them wake up.'

She was feeling terribly uneasy standing helplessly in the middle of a room littered with unconscious or hopefully dead demons. She looked down at her locator which indicated she was in the right place to find the keys.

"They should be here," she whispered to herself.

The vault had shelves and shelves of ancient books, star charts, maps and all kinds of instruments that seemed divinely inspired. In the centre of the opposite wall was a map that reminded Liberty of Riverdale. It looked similar to a plan view of Riverdale, but there seemed to be other roads running through buildings, and a massive building in the heart of the city. Then she recognised that the map was showing underground as well as surface detail. In the centre of the map was a hand-drawn 'X' with the two words 'altar' and 'keys.' The word 'keys' had a couple of underlines.

'The large building must be where the altar is. An enormous building underground!' she thought.

She scanned the map to find the library, where she thought she was and saw that there was quite some distance between her and the 'X' on the altar.

As she looked over various objects in the room, her eyes came to rest on a giant slab of stone crafted into a table, on which was laid out a huge collection of keys.

'This is what I've come for,' she thought. 'How on earth am I to find the keys to the city in the midst of all these?'

The keys were of all shapes and sizes. Some looked old, rusted and worn. Others looked like metallic circuit boards, cut to fit a slot in a computer. There were others that were like cut glass, with lines and shapes engraved into them. She reached out her hand to begin to sift through the mass. As she did so her locator started to hum. She moved her hand across the keys again, more slowly this time. The hum increased or decreased in volume in response to her movements. Reasoning that the locator had not only led her to the vault but would also show her the exact keys, she started to explore the collection on the table by sweeping her hand slowly over them. She returned her hand to where the hum was loudest and picked up a collection of keys. Most were shaped in a rectangle, slightly larger than a credit card. As she sifted through the keys, it dawned on her that she had no idea what the keys to the altar looked like; they were all so different.

"God show me," she said picking up key after key. Her locator continued to hum. As she looked at her locator again, she remembered the buttons on the side. She pressed the button that had produced the dim light, casting soft highlights and shadows over the table. As the light fell over the keys, two keys that were next to each other responded to the light as if a chemical reaction had taken place. Their edges glowed, and so did the detailing engraved into them.

"These are the ones!" she said with confidence as she lifted them from their place in amongst the collection.

"Useful after all," she said to her locator as she patted the button which had turned on the light. Grateful for completing that part of her mission, she relaxed a little and inspected some of the other keys. She picked one up that looked like a giant microchip which reflected the light along its edges. Another looked well-worn like an ancient artefact from some long-forgotten civilisation. As she picked up and inspected other keys that caught her attention, she heard footsteps just on the other side of the door that she had entered. Liberty dove under the table and quickly bagged all the keys she had in her hands.

She felt a presence enter the room, an uncomfortable presence. Unable to see what it was from her vantage point, she moved her head a little to get a better look. All she could see was light from the other side of the table. Liberty's heart was racing. She was hardly breathing, trying to be as quiet as possible. Her leg started to get a cramp from being crouched under the table. The pain in her leg got worse as the seconds ticked by, so she adjusted her position. As she moved, her foot bumped the desk. The sound of the grind of the table leg on the stone floor made her heart jump. Her hopes of remaining unseen suddenly dashed as a large set of keys fell from the table and clattered to the stone paving. Immediately she leaped out of her hiding place with sword drawn and lunged toward the other end of the room.

"Stop!" said a voice behind her. The voice did not sound angry or alarmed; rather the voice sounded like it could have come from one of the angels that she had already met.

Liberty spun around, poised to defend herself but a glorious radiance filled her eyes. There stood a beautiful angel. Sparks emitted from his presence like miniature stars being formed and then fading into the shadows. Witnessing the entire life-cycle of stars being born and then dying within a matter seconds was captivating to watch. Surely this creature was a mighty angel, designed for significant assignments.

"Well done!" he said. "You have the keys, you have completed your quest."

"Have I?" said Liberty bewildered. "Don't I have to return these keys to the altar to realign the mission of this city?"

"Certainly." The angel paused and considered her. "That must be done and shall be done. I will carry these myself and return them to the altar. Your part of the mission was to retrieve the keys, and you have displayed courage, skill, and faith. Well done. The other two teams are just about to complete, so we must return these keys quickly, and I can do this in an instant. You may come with me if you like."

Liberty breathed a sigh of relief, "Thank you for coming. I'm so glad that the other teams are doing so well."

She reached into her bag to hand over the keys, but as she did, she felt uneasy. 'This isn't quite right,' she thought. She remembered the words of the angel who commissioned her, "This task is for you, and you alone must return the keys to their rightful place." A little panic started to rise within her. She moved her hand to the side pocket of her bag and drew out the two keys that were in the pocket, then slowly walked over to the angel and gave them to him. The angel stepped back. The stars that she had been admiring began to die off quickly around him.

"Thank you," he said. "I shall now return these to where they belong."

The angel smiled, but it didn't bring her any comfort. 'I don't like that smile anymore,' thought Liberty, 'I'm in danger!' The angel started to turn dark. The growing state of panic caused her cheeks to feel flushed, and a band of worried tightness spread across her forehead. A verse flashed through her mind, 'Satan himself masquerades as an angel of light.' She lifted her eyes, again to meet his eyes and in a moment of full realisation of who she was looking at, she then turned and fled in horror. A door at the opposite end of the room was ahead of her. Glancing backward, she saw that the angel wasn't moving and wasn't chasing her, but his hand stretched out in her direction. A dark power swirled around his arm. 'He's about to hit me with darkness!' she thought.

"Oh God help me!" she cried out. Adrenaline surged through her limbs, but her mind was moving quicker than her body. "Move!" she commanded her legs, but they seemed to be moving in slow motion. Everything appeared to slow down as she realised that she had a minimal chance of escape. With all of her energy, she burst through the door and out of the vault.

"Quick, in here!" resounded the voice of Falcon. Liberty felt a firm grip embrace her arm and yanked her sideways. As her body jerked to the left, a sickening darkness blew past her face and devoured a wall beside her. She stared at the gaping hole aghast as Falcon dragged her into a room off the passageway. The hole dripped with slimy emptiness. It looked like a portal into the blackness of hell… and it probably was.

31

The Throne
- Mission Girls -

The girls were still high in the sky. As they looked down, they could see a river that ran through the middle of the ranks like an iridescent ribbon of light blue silk, dividing the plain into two. Originating from a powerful spring at the rear of the army, it cut a channel the entire length of the plain and over the edge of Grace Falls. Not far from the place where the water cascaded over the cliff was a wide stone bridge that spanned the river. The sturdy cobbled bridge looked like it had been set in place long ago. The worn blocks of stone that had been weathered by the ages were fitted together to create the archway over the waters. Two stone pillars stood at each end of the bridge, draped with ropes and flags flapping in the breeze. The banners were dark, embroidered with strange symbols.

'Those are enemy flags,' thought Samantha, 'Claiming Grace Falls as theirs, no doubt.'

The bridge looked like it belonged to a grand entrance of a castle.

Samantha imagined that it had carried many horses and knights across it over the centuries. Warriors returning after epic battles, seeking an audience with great kings to claim their reward, would have set foot upon it.

'And demons too!' she thought with disgust. The presence of them contaminated the scene that she was imagining.

In the centre of the bridge was the throne, set in stone. As Trinity looked at the throne, she saw a large, obese demon upon it. This creature was the one whom they had been sent to eradicate. It sat in a slouched position with an oversized crown on its head, unsuited to the royal surroundings that it inhabited.

"There's our target," called Seraph as he pointed towards the one on the throne. "We must destroy it, and then the hordes will disperse. The lifeline of demons is a fragile thread. Once the thread gets severed, they lose all power. The basis of their strength is lies, delusions, and deception." Seraph continued, "Truth is a rock which stands firm forever. When truth confronts a lie, the lie is exposed, and the thread gets cut. So once we destroy that which sits on the throne, all the other demons connected to it will lose their power and will be dispersed, back to where they came from to get reassigned."

"Though, if we happen to take some demons out on our way to the throne..." said Trillion with a smile, "they fade out of this realm and find themselves in the abyss."

"The more the better I say," said Trinity.

"We must be careful, we have nearly reached the goal of our mission," said Seraph. "One of you must kill the demon on the throne because it is you who carry faith. Trillion and I will charge first and make a path for you. You will follow us closely behind. Then use whatever you find in your hands to assault the throne, and destroy that demon."

"What happens if you get hit? What happens if we get shot or sliced?" Samantha asked anxiously, trying to keep her nerves at bay.

"If one of us gets hit, we return to the Lord and are reassigned. If you get hit you drop out of this realm, and we fail the assignment. Hold your faith. Do not worry. Come, let us go!"

The two angels swooped down, both holding swords in each hand. The girls did not reach for weapons because their wings followed their arm movements and they needed to maintain their flight path towards the throne. As they got closer to the hordes, the scene below became more chaotic. The cacophony of noise coming from the multitude arguing, hissing and spitting would help to conceal any alert that a demon may want to make. As the four glided towards the bridge and the throne below, several demons looked up and screeched. The masses didn't take notice because of the chaos around them. But some nearby turned and looked upward in disgust and rose into the sky from the ranks with swords and shields at the ready. Trillion and Seraph wielded their swords as arrows shot towards them. Trillion slashed through two arrows as they flew past his left side. The girls were close now. The activity below them became more and more intense. Other demons rose to defend their leader. The girls were nearly at the bridge when a stray arrow pierced Trinity's wing. She fell. As she hit the ground, she rolled to break her fall and manoeuvred herself into a standing position. Samantha also touched down as a blade slashed through one of her wings. The wings crumbled away, and the girls were free to draw weapons and run. They raced towards the throne, slashing and cutting their way through the ranks. Other demons were closing in, almost upon them. Suddenly two beams of spinning laser light flashed past them, destroying a dozen demons who were closest to them, creating a path to run through. Liberty's prayer had struck its mark. The faith of Samantha and Trinity soared.

An enemy landed just in front of Samantha. Without breaking her stride she flung one of her swords at the demon, but it raised its blade and fended off the attack, sending the sword flying away into the army. Samantha prepared herself for a close-range encounter. The demon got agitated as she advanced. Her faith continued to rise, overpowering her enemy. As she came within range, she struck the blade from its hand and brought her sword down on her enemy, with supernatural force, splitting it in half.

The angels landed on either side of the girls, swords blazing. More demons were alerted. Trinity and Samantha stepped up onto the bridge, focused on the task ahead. Sensing their presence the enthroned demon turned its head and glared at them with rage in its eyes. The beast lifted its heavy arm, suspended it in the air for a moment then slammed its hand on the armrest. As it did, a shockwave went out from the throne and knocked the girls off their feet sending them flying off the bridge. They hit the ground hard and slid along the gravel. Samantha raised her head off the dirt, physically shaken from the impact. All she could hear was ringing in her ears. Her vision was blurry, and she couldn't think straight. Demons were lying beside her. 'They also must have been taken out by the blast,' she thought. Lifting her head higher, she looked through her matted hair and saw more demons advancing on them. Her body throbbed. She hardly had the strength to lift herself up.

"We're not going to make it," shouted Samantha. "God, help!"

32

BRIDGE
- MISSION LIBERTY -

Falcon pulled Liberty into a side room just in time as the darkness blew past her, blasting a slimy portal of blackness through the wall. He slammed the door shut and whacked down a bar to lock the door in place.

"He is already here. Our time is short," said Falcon.

"Who is here?" questioned Liberty.

"The one who suffered defeat at the cross. You must retrieve the keys that you handed over and then get them to the altar, but I fear that we may have lost now that they are securely in the enemy's hands," said Falcon.

Liberty reached into her sash, "You mean these keys?" she said as she lifted the keys of the city into view.

Falcon's expression was one of relief and wonder, "But how?"

"I just took a couple of extra ones that I liked the look of and handed those keys over instead of these. I knew that I must fulfil this mission myself."

"Good girl," he said extremely relieved. Falcon was impressed by the presence of mind that the human girl had displayed to handover fake keys. "This is why God chose you. Now go, I must stay here and face whatever may come." Falcon reached out and adjusted Liberty's locator. He set it to the location of the altar.

"You must return these keys to Mission Altar, located in the heart of the city, deep underground. If by the time you lock the keys into place, the throne is secure and the Elemental Stone is free, the return of the keys will, at that moment, free the city."

"Continue along this walkway. After you have gone on for about half a mile, you will open out into another chamber. You will see some stairs that go down to your right into darkness. Do not be afraid, but have your sword ready. At the bottom of the stairs on the opposite wall, there will be a lever that you will need to pull all the way down to its furthest extent, which will extend a bridge out over the expanse towards the inner sanctuary. You will then be able to walk through the inner sanctuary to the altar in the centre. I would like to be there with you, but you must do this alone. Move quickly; you have little time."

The urgency of the moment escalated as the door that Falcon had locked started to rumble and shake. It began to glow red hot and looked as though it would give way at any moment. Liberty nodded to Falcon, then dashed off along the tunnel. Behind her, she heard an explosion and her heart skipped a beat, but she didn't turn around, knowing that she had to keep moving forward. A passage of scripture flashed across her mind about Lot's wife becoming a pillar of salt.

"Don't worry, I'm not looking!" she called out, raising her gaze heavenward for a moment as she ran.

The walkway was narrow which was comforting because it limited the possibility of an enemy attack to only in front of her or behind her. 'Surely they know I'm here,' she thought. 'How much further? I must be nearly to the first chamber by now,' recalling her track & field days. As she ran, an unpleasant aroma filled the air, almost causing her to gag. Then all of a sudden a tall skinny creature stepped out in front of her and blocked her path. Liberty recognised the hideous creature from the beginning of her journey. It was the one from Grolg's Ravine who had flown it to check on the others.

"It's you," the creature hissed as it stepped out from an opening in the corridor. "I've been looking for you!"

Liberty felt her heart beat rapidly increasing, then heard a quiet calm voice in her spirit, "I've not given you a spirit of fear, but of power, love and a sound mind. Have strength, my child." Power rose up inside of her, and she reached for the small knife strapped to her thigh.

'I walk by faith,' she said to herself, 'If God is for me, who can be against me.' Liberty was grateful that she knew her scripture. She controlled her breathing and stood up straight, challenging the creature. Her confidence surprised the demon who expected her to cower in fear. This demon only traded in fear and pride; it did not know how to handle faith. It possessed no weapon that could stand against the faith of a true believer. Liberty started to walk towards it. Her face was resolute, staring down the demon. She picked up speed and broke into a run towards it. The creature's face started to twitch, it already knew it had lost, even before Liberty's knife pierced its skin. The creature dropped to its knees, stunned that the faith of a mere girl had stripped him of power. Liberty threw her knife which hit its mark and stuck fast between its ribs. As she ran past, she drew back her fist gave it a blow to the head. The demon was knocked over and hit the floor as Liberty continued along the corridor without slowing down.

She came out into the expanse and saw the stairs down to her right. With sword drawn, she quickly stepped down into thick darkness. The stairs continued to go deeper and deeper into the heart of the earth. On her right was a rocky wall that she could place her hand on to steady herself as she quickly descended. A gentle breeze blew through the open expanse to her left. She could see nothing, but in the midst of the darkness she heard sounds, murmurings, and echoes, but she remained focused. Down and down she went for minutes and minutes.

She stumbled as she stomped her foot on the ground, expecting to drop down to another stair. At last, she had made it to the deepest level. All was darkness, so she decided to use her locator light on her wrist. The gentle glow was enough for her eyes to adjust. Just in front of her was the lever on the wall that Falcon had mentioned. She reached out her hand to pull it down. In response, a sliding sound of grinding stone could be heard rumbling through the darkness. A bridge slowly slid out to the left of her. She crouched down, waiting for it to extend the whole way over the expanse. It took extra time that she didn't feel she had. Impatiently she looked around, to see if she could detect any danger. Murmurings still echoed around her, but she had no idea how far away the creatures were that were making the noises. The bridge continued to reach out over the chasm slowly. Finally, the bridge spanned the gap between her and a doorway on the far side. There was no time to waste; she just wanted this over.

Just as she was about to step foot onto the bridge, a prompting caused her to stop and pray.

"Lord, protect me, keep me safe and help me to do this." As she did, renewed faith rose in her heart and the 'shield of faith' appeared strapped to her arm.

"Go," she told herself and made a run for it across the bridge and into the open expanse. All seemed to be going well until a whipping sounded through the air. She raised her shield as two arrows glanced off it. Another struck the bridge in front of her. Liberty stopped and crouched down, getting as much of her body behind the shield as possible. Her vitals were protected by the shield, but she couldn't pull her boots in far enough to avoid a direct hit. An arrow penetrated her thick boot and the tip stuck into her foot just below her ankle. She let out a yell of pain and immediately yanked it out, throwing it off the edge of the bridge. Liberty scrunched her eyes and opened her mouth and a faint cry passed between her lips. She clutched her foot with tears rolling down her cheeks. There she was, suspended in the middle of an expanse on a narrow bridge with a boot moistening with her blood. 'God it hurts! How many are there and where are they?' Liberty was aware that only one side had protection at a time. Two more arrows came from her left. Liberty instinctively swung the shield over her back to the other side to block them, and they sheered off her shield.

Liberty was stuck and hurting, she didn't want to stand up and expose her body to more arrows. She waited. 'God help me. What am I going to do?' Liberty remained in a crouched position, feeling more and more helpless. Suddenly she felt the bridge jolt like a sharp earthquake had struck. The bridge then began to rumble, and she saw a piece of it break off and fall into the blackness below. Then another piece of the bridge broke free in front of her and dropped out of sight.

"What's happening?"

"Go!" she felt God say to her. "Go now!"

"I can't. I can't move!"

Then, in a flash, by revelation, God showed her that this bridge was held together by faith. As she had waited, a gradual entrance of fear had been permitted by her and was slowly creeping through her heart and also through the structure of the bridge. Fear was growing through the rock beneath her like tree roots extending into the earth. As the dark fingers pushed their way through the bridge, it began to break up and become unstable.

She picked herself up and continued to run with her foot screaming at her to stop, but she found that through gritted teeth she could keep moving. More arrows assailed her, but the shield was doing its job. Nearing the end of the bridge, she slung the shield over her back, now that the goal was in sight. Another two arrows hit the shield jolting her forward.

"Nearly there!" she told herself, instinctively ducking as another arrow careered over her head.

"Wow! That was close!"

Liberty ran to the door, reached for the handle, pulled it open and dashed through in one quick movement slamming the door behind her. The slam echoed around her and then faded off to silence.

33

ARROW

- mission girls -

Meanwhile, Layla had been grounded and remained on the ledge. Shar launched into the air to advance on their attackers. Layla continued to run past more windows. 'I wonder if I should run back and get some more wings?' she considered for a moment. Deciding that forward was better than backward, she continued along the ledge. More windows passed by with verses inscribed upon them. Just then a demon landed in front of her. She drew her bow and shot it through the chest. As it fell, Layla stepped over it and continued to move forward. More demons began to land on the path that Layla was on with their eyes trained on her. 'Running out of options,' she thought. Startled by the arrival of two more directly behind her, she turned and dived into a window, just catching the scripture reference as she flew through – Acts 8:39-40.

She landed hard on a smooth, polished surface and slid along the floor. She quickly got up and spun around to face whatever may follow her. She waited a moment, but none pursued. She slowly turned to sweep the room with her gaze to see if there was anything useful. Again, the circular room was bare. The most interesting part of the room was the ceiling which had richly ornamented engravings of battle scenes, landscapes, and maps. In the centre was a dome that lit the room. As she studied the ceiling, she could see that all the engraving and patterns splayed out from the light in the centre. She found herself drawn to its glow. Layla walked into the middle of the room so that she stood directly under the dome and gazed up at it. The light did not hurt her eyes but brought into sharp focus some words inscribed on the stonework around it. As she read, she recognised the portion of scripture from Acts.

'When they came up out of the water, the Spirit of the Lord suddenly took Philip away, and the eunuch did not see him again, but went on his way rejoicing. Philip, however, appeared at Azotus and travelled about, preaching the gospel in all the towns until he reached Caesarea.'

'Transported,' said Layla to herself, 'The Spirit took him away and placed him somewhere else.' Then almost knowing what might happen next, she stood directly under the light and took half a step backward so that her feet stood shoulder length apart. As she reached out a hand, an arrow materialised between her fingers and thumb. Layla then raised her bow, set the arrow against the string and pulled back. The string touched her lips, and she closed one eye, poised to release.

***

Samantha and Trinity looked up at the throne, feeling helpless, realising that any moment they could drop out of the vision with their task uncompleted. They frantically glanced around looking for angels or anyone who would step in to help. As they turned to face the edge of the cliff about fifty metres away, next to the river's edge, what looked like a person appeared right before their eyes. Mist that rose from the falls framed the silhouette of a strong feminine figure poised in a confident battle-stance. Could this person be the intervention of God that the girls right now so desperately needed? Trinity squinted her eyes and could just make out that the figure had a drawn bow pointed directly towards the throne.

"Layla!" shouted Trinity, recognising her friend.

Layla breathed out a half breath to still any nonessential movement in her body. She focused on the occupant of the throne. The scene before her reflected off the wet glassy surface of her eyes. The atmosphere over the falls was dark. The wind had picked up, and it was cold. Thick cloud cover had swept in, and it had started to rain. The noise of the enemy faded into the background as she concentrated on the one shot that she was about to take. She could hear her heartbeat slowing in her ears. Layla's gaze narrowed a little. She took one last moment to aim, then released the string of the bow from her fingers. As the arrow was set free, the string twanged back into position, Layla's outstretched arm remained stable pointing toward her target. The arrow shot dead straight from the bow. The stabilising feathers brushed the surface of the wood of the bow as the arrow slid past with deadly accuracy. The arrow sailed through the air with the momentum of faith behind it. It cut through raindrops, pierced the mist, and plunged into the stomach of the one on the throne. The demon slumped forward. The heavily jewelled crown it had been wearing fell from its head and clanged on to the bridge at the foot of the throne. The demon slowly tipped forward under its weight and tumbled to the ground. Moments later the demon faded out, its influence erased from the realm.

The ranks behind the throne let out an awful moan as they instantly felt the sudden loss of their leader. Howls and groans went up from the hordes. From her vantage point, Layla surveyed the battleground. She saw a heavily armoured demon stretch out its arms, tensing its muscles, roaring like an angry lion. It was clutching a chain with a spiked ball with one hand and held a shield with the other. As it stood, parts of the demon began to dissolve into flakes, like burnt paper being whisked away by the wind. The body that had once held up the armour strapped on to it was hollowing out, and pieces of armour and weaponry fell to the ground. The ball and chain dropped to the gravel. Without a master, the weapon became as useless as scrap metal in a forgotten junkyard, isolated, and never again used to engage in battle. Across the entire army, each demon was erased like fallen leaves swept away by an Autumn breeze. Enemy dust rose into the darkened skies as the plain emptied out. Soon just Trinity, Samantha, Trillion and Seraph were left on the deserted battlefield with Layla still standing on the edge of the cliff from where she had shot the arrow.

***

The throne began to regain its golden colour and shine. As the throne shone brighter and brighter, the waters beneath it were restored to their original deep blue colour. All of a sudden, a rush of sapphire-blue flooded the waters and cascaded over the falls. A rich sapphire hue rushed through all of the water channels in the city. Rich blue pathways cut through the city and seeped into the waters under the ground. A wall of blue light reached skyward and intersected the Elemental Axis in the centre of the city.

***

Trinity and Samantha raced along the edge of the river towards Layla. They embraced each other tightly, praising God for their safety and for winning the throne for their city.

Trinity, Samantha, and Layla from their location at the throne saw the red flash from Razor Peak and the skies clearing. They raised their arms in joy.

"Yes! Victory!" shouted Trinity. "They must have done it!"

The boys could neither see nor hear the girls but saw the sapphire glow of the throne over the falls.

"Check that out!" exclaimed Tristan.

"Ha! They've secured the throne!" shouted Caden and slapped Tristan a high-five. The axes could clearly be seen, reaching high into the sky. The red axis ran west to east, intersecting the blue axis running north to south.

***

All eyes then looked towards the centre of the city wondering about Liberty and her mission, praying that she would be successful. Hers was the last part of their collective quest.

34

BEYOND THE VISION
- MISSION LIBERTY -

Liberty stood with her back to the door gasping for breath. She had made it into the inner sanctuary, to the very centre of the foundations of the city. By the grace of God, she had made it! As her breathing calmed, she took the time to study the new environment that she had just entered. The sanctuary was massive, the size of a football field. She saw the altar, a sole object, situated in the middle of the expansive floor space. The altar sat on a hexagonal platform that stood ten feet high. Six steps on each side of the platform led up to the altar. A dusky light shone directly down upon it.

The vault was cold. A thick mist covered the floor almost to Liberty's knees. Higher up, wisps of mist hung in the air. The ceiling of the vault was a huge canopy of rock arching over to form a dome above the altar. The light upon the altar came from a thin cross of light cut through the middle of the ceiling. It was too dark to make out much more detail than that, but as she traced her gaze down to eye-level and her eyes adjusted, she noticed shadowy openings into the sanctuary like stadium entrances, spaced evenly around the perimeter.

There was a lot of open ground to cover. Her foot was throbbing. 'It's time to have real faith!' she thought. 'Nothing can stop me from completing this quest. If God is with me who can be against me!'

Liberty looked down at her boot that was shrouded in mist and spoke to it, "You will not cause me pain! Pain, you have no place here in Jesus name. Foot be healed. You will hold together until I complete this mission!" Liberty decided to give no more thought to her wounded foot. She had prayed and that was enough. She didn't even let a hint of feeling sorry for herself creep in. Too many people fall in to that trap and take too long to get out of it. Faith is a decision, a decision to be victorious, a decision to be free.

Liberty turned her thoughts back to the sanctuary. She would be in plain sight. But her mission felt achievable now that she could see the altar. Liberty tensed, ready to make the final dash for the completion of her assignment. Liberty took a last look, scanning the area. The sanctuary was empty and quiet. Stepping out in faith, she made a run for it. Nothing else could be heard apart from the tap, tap, tap of her boots striking the floor. The rhythmic tapping of her footsteps echoed around the vault. A single soul, crossing a lonely expanse, running with fluid motions like an athlete, intent on winning a gold medal. At that moment nothing else mattered.

Suddenly demons rushed out from every opening into the sanctuary, savagely focused on her demise. Liberty continued to run but the enemy was closing in, they were coming in too fast. Hundreds were pouring into the sanctuary like an army of ants covering the ground in blackness. Her once clear path of opportunity was closing to a narrow gap. Soon she would be surrounded. How could she possibly defeat so many? How could the mission closing in so quickly when she had come so far? Her faith was still holding at this, the final hour. More and more demons rushed in like a flood.

"Liberty," she heard clearly. A verse dropped into her heart.

'Now to him who is able to do immeasurably more than all we ask or imagine, according to his power that is at work within us, to him be glory in the church and in Christ Jesus throughout all generations, forever and ever!'

'That's it!' she thought. Instantly it became alive within her – a 'rhema' – a direct word from God. 'God, you can do immeasurably more than all I could ask or imagine.' She claimed the victory in her heart. Right then, as she reached a point of revelation, her surroundings changed. The ambient light that lit the sanctuary drew in towards her. It was like an implosion of light, with her in the very centre. She grew to eight feet tall. Her strength, agility, and understanding heightened to that of a fully released child of God, freed from earthly limitations. Time stood still, allowing this revelation to penetrate every part of her being. She transformed.

Another verse flashed into her mind.

'And God raised us up with Christ and seated us with him in the heavenly realms in Christ Jesus.'

"I am seated deep within the centre of the heavenly realms. I am above this battle. You have no substance," she declared to the enemy who shared her space.

Liberty saw that the demons and her surroundings were able to be swept away. They are all just forms of mist. She then understood that her mission was not at all ending in defeat. The mission itself wasn't what it seemed to be. For all of them, for Tristan, Caden, Layla, Samantha, Trinity and herself, the mission was not a journey through the battle-field of a city, but rather a journey into themselves. The journey of discovering and releasing faith. God had triumphed over the battle before she was even born. Jesus had won the victory at the cross, and all she needed to do was to enforce his victory through absolute faith and obedience.

As a child of God, she could partner with God just by standing firm. Through this partnership, she could command her environment to conform and align to the will of God.

Liberty questioned, 'God are you wanting me, enticing me, daring me, even expecting me to move the fabric of the universe around me? Is all of this temporary and malleable?'

As her reasoning continued, she became more confident in what she believed. 'Our boundaries are not set by time and space, but by our faith in what God can do. Jesus taught that with a simple command, a mountain could be lifted off its foundations and cast into the sea. Matter can be displaced. Jesus himself commanded the storm to cease, and taught that she could do the same. Nothing would be impossible for her. The physical laws are under the jurisdiction of the people of God. 'Time' was even reversed by God, through Isaiah, in Hezekiah's days.'

'I have been born into the environment of faith. Angels and demons are not born into that realm and therefore have not the ability to bend the laws. But because I am in God's image, seated in heavenly places with Christ, I can influence even where angels and demons find their limits. Thank you, Lord, for revealing this to me.'

Liberty immediately saw the opposite perspective from what she had seen all along, the secret to winning her city! When she had first stepped into the spirit realm, she thought that earth was subject to the atmosphere of the spirit world. But her perspective now reversed. She had thought that what happened in the spirit affected the surface. But the greater truth is that the realm of angels and demons look to the church to see what the church will do. The spirit realm waits to see whether a Christian will step out in faith or hold back in fear. Whether there is confidence in the Lord or doubt, determines what is permitted and what is forbidden in the local atmosphere.

'His intent was that now, through the church, the manifold wisdom of God should be made known to the rulers and authorities in the heavenly realms...'

Liberty realised that the entire spiritual realm of her city looked to her, waiting, would she have faith or would she allow the enemy to smother her. It is people, God's sons and daughters, who primarily determine the atmosphere around them. They lead, the spirit follows. They either give power to the light or strength to the darkness. The surface is the real battleground. It is in the hands of God's children.

Jesus died on the cross and rose from the dead, conquering the enemy. Because Jesus won the war, he has given Christians the ability to win their battles. These battles are won by Christians on the surface first; then the spirit realm can act within the parameters set for them by the release of faith.

Liberty realised that the victory was already in her heart. Her enemy didn't stand a chance against her. She had faith, she had a revelation, and the Spirit of God within her.

All these thoughts exploded in her mind as the revelation unravelled in less than a second.

Her eyes blazed with blue fire. In each hand appeared a sword, lit with glowing verses of scripture engraved along the blade. The scriptures were like thin flames of fire that danced across the surface of each blade. She stretched her arms straight out to the left and right. Liberty saw through the fabric of the vision and into the creator's architectural framework. Her surroundings changed, from the grey that she had been traveling through, to a stripped-back, open white canvas with black lines and curves detailing the structure of the room and of the demons that were assailing her. A more pure reality. She saw every detail of the dimensional space of her surroundings in crystal clear focus like looking at intricate sketches of black on white. In an instant, she saw the framework of every foe all at once.

Liberty sprang forward moving her arms in beautiful arcs with graceful, powerful movements, slashing countless enemies. Her blades stretched out to unnatural distances, decapitating scores of enemies like a giant sickle harvesting a field of wheat in a single stroke. Every movement, purposeful and precise. Arcs of light accompanied her movements as she spun and slashed her way towards the altar.

'Still got a lot of ground to cover,' she thought, 'I don't have time for this.'

In one graceful leap, she soared high over her enemy and cleared the remaining distance as if given the ability to fly. As she glided through the air, she released the swords from her hands with a flick. The swords spun to the ground, discharging arcs of light in all directions, flattening the enemy. While in the air, Liberty slid her backpack over her head. As the pack sailed in front of her, the keys slipped out, and she caught one in each hand.

The mist rolled away from her as she landed at the base of the steps. Just then, a bright blue beam of light cut through the room and shone across the altar. Then almost immediately, a deep red beam of light cut through the sanctuary from the opposite direction and intersected the blue beam at the central point of the altar. She knew instantly that these were the Elemental and Throne axes released to life by the other teams. Two slots on the top of the altar opened up.

Without hesitation, she walked up the steps and slid the keys into the slots. A release of energy splayed out, washed down the steps and as it hit the floor, shot upwards like an upward waterfall completely engulfing the altar, the stairs, and Liberty. It was a burning pillar of energy drawn skyward. The sound was like a raging ocean with the breakers smashing into a rugged coastline. Liberty remained with her hands on the altar steadying herself in the midst of the eruption. As she stood within the stormy pillar, fearful demons were being drawn into it as if a vortex had taken hold of them. Demons got vaporised as they came too close. Any loose stones or bricks from the wall of the sanctuary were dislodged and hurtled towards the centre of the expanse. The entire vault looked like it may implode as anything that was not anchored securely was ripped from its place. All remaining demons got erased from the realm.

As the energy stabilised into a pillar of smooth light, the echoes of the initial explosion faded away. The light then expanded to fill the entire vault. Liberty felt warmth all around her as if submerged in warm, soothing oil. All became peaceful. All became still apart from the steady surge of the pillar in the centre of the city.

Liberty stood alone, in the silence. She then dropped to her knees, suddenly exhausted, and thanked the Lord for completion.

35

COMPLETION
- MISSION LIBERTY -

The mission was complete. Above her head, Liberty heard the grinding of stone on stone. She looked up and saw that the roof was dividing into quarters, sliding outwards. The cross-shaped opening was widening. As more of the night sky became revealed, light from the altar burst upwards in powerful waves of energy. Flashes of light ignited the skies above. The central column looked as bright as the sun. After a few moments her eyes grew accustomed, and she was able to gaze into it.

Out from the central column, rivers of light flowed upwards towards the heavens. The rivers curved and arced through the skies. As they ascended, the curves and bends in the rivers released sparks and splashes of colour. The splashes formed geometric patterns at various elevations, accentuating the vastness and depth of the skies above the city. Patterns crisscrossed each other forming cascading fractals. Rivers of glory lit the clouds, filling the sky with magnificent 'archi-texture,' an 'atmos-fusion' of spiritual and natural, representing the partnership of men and women with God. Droplets of glory rained down on the city, alighting on the inhabitants.

From Razor Peak, Caden and Tristan saw the brilliance.

"She's done it!" cried Caden. "She got to the altar!"

Suddenly a moment of revelation dawned on Tristan, 'Those are my colours – the blue and the red that I see in my visions!' he thought.

From Grace Falls, Layla, Samantha, and Trinity followed the glory trails with their eyes. The brilliance reflected off their armour. Their eyes shone as they gazed at the exploding light in the skies. Smiles lit each of the girl's faces as they stood captivated by what they saw. It was evident that Liberty had succeeded.

Layla didn't speak; there was nothing to say. Her soul felt refreshed and energised by the glory that rained down. As the droplets splashed on her head, drenching her hair, the rain seemed to seep into her being, trickling down her insides, watering her soul. She basked in the glory, delighting in the beauty of a city, drawn into alignment under God.

Samantha lifted her hands to let the glory splash onto her palms. Rain fell from the sky and as it hit the ground showers of droplets fell back into the sky again unhindered by regular gravitational forces. Her heart was full of joy, yet she also felt humbled that she had contributed to the release of the rains. Trinity felt the approval of God within her.

God spoke into her heart, "Congratulations good and faithful servant. You have displayed faith and courage, in the face of imminent danger. You have placed others ahead of yourself and shown the love of God through your actions."

As Trinity considered God's message to her, she glanced at the faces of the others and knew they too felt the seal of the Lord's approval and affection.

***

Liberty stood up and reached out her hands heavenward. The light drew her in and up into the slip-stream. She rose above the city in the midst of the light and rested in the glorious power that carried her. All around her was brilliance.

Then the other three girls and the two boys were also lifted off their feet and raised high into the sky. All six were now high above the city. They could see the red axis running west to east across the city. They could see the blue axis running north to south, intersecting at the altar. The golden axis rose vertically from the altar and splayed out over the city like a dome.

The six were lifted together into the sky, into the midst of the trails of light. The angel with the four faces joined them - the one who had briefed them at the beginning. He drew them higher into the earth's atmosphere so that the entire country came into view. Riverdale reduced to a bright point of light like a star gracing the night sky. From the city, four beams of light shot out, connecting Riverdale with four sister cities across the country. The networks looked much like the constellations mapped out across the expanse of space. These four cities also had alignment.

Along with the bright spots, there were also dark patches distorting the country-scape. These cities did not have alignment. The dark cities also had sister cities with dark trails connecting them.

'How beautiful is this!' thought Samantha, 'It's like looking at satellite imagery. All the sparkling cities and the connections between them encompassed by the long ribbon of coastline. It's the spiritual map of my country!'

For a moment they became stationary, suspended between heaven and earth.

The angel spoke, "As a city becomes restored, it connects with other 'God Cities.' Angelic highways form, and God's kingdom advances. All over the world, every day, new relationships are being forged, and others are damaged. But God's kingdom continues to strengthen over the earth. The planet we call Earth, God's pearl, orbiting around his purposes, is being won and will eventually completely come into alignment. But not until the end."

As Liberty considered the size of the globe and the obvious contrast of dark versus light stretched over the surface, she realised that they were a part of something much bigger. Her city was one spark on earth that blazed on a fluid, ever-changing surface. Cities were steadily being won and lost, growing or decreasing in brightness over time. To Liberty, the bright spots were reminiscent of the moving waters of the ocean on a sunny day with sunlight reflecting off the crest of waves causing them to sparkle like golden droplets. Dark areas floated over the surface of the earth, like shadows being cast by ever-shifting clouds, only to be cleared away allowing cities to sparkle once again. The scene in front of her started to change. The earth began to spin faster, and Liberty realised that she was looking at earth's history spanning hundreds of years. The spread of sparkles grew, then receded, but then expanded again to cover more of the surface.

***

The angel took them higher still. The earth that once filled their vision became a sphere, a ball in space. The six continued their journey away and out. The light faded, blackness took over. As the brilliance slipped away, the walls of Liberty's lounge room appeared around her.

***

She was back in her lounge, where she had begun to pray earlier that evening. She looked up at the clock on the wall, 12.46am. 'I've been in that vision for days and days, but here it has only been a few hours!'

'Was that real? Did we align our city?' thought Liberty, desperately seeking confirmation that she wasn't just dreaming. Emotions of achievement and accomplishment remained within her like a banner of victory in her heart, but reasoning started to cloud her feelings with the depressive reality that the whole adventure could have been entirely within her mind. Logic and reason were unwelcome companions at that moment.

'God, don't leave me alone!' she called out from within the depths her soul. She slowly turned to survey the familiar objects that were in the room. The new family portrait hung on the wall, taken a couple of weeks before. It was a candid photograph with her parents to one side, her dad with his arm around her mum. Liberty was turned side-on, piggy-backing her younger brother, both with broad grins. The portrait brought a smile to her face. She continued to gaze around the room. The same old wall cabinet that contained statues, cups, shells and bits and pieces from her parent's international travels, stood out as a feature of the room. Then she caught a glimpse of herself in the mirror and gasped. She still wore her armour. She reached down, gripping the hilt, and drew out her sword. She slowly moved the blade through the air. As she did, it slowly faded into mist as did the armour. Angel-Light weaved past and drew her attention. The light grew more intense as it moved around her room. Angel-Light spun together and formed an angel right in front of her eyes.

"Falcon!" she said.

"Yes Liberty," Falcon replied smiling, answering her silent questions. "You and your friends have succeeded. The culmination of the faith journey of each member of your team, along with much prayer, has brought about this amazing restoration. The throne is ours, the atmosphere is ours, and you have revived the city's mission. Riverdale will remember its purpose. The scene is all set for the crusade ahead. There is no doubt; it will be a success."

The others also returned to where they had been. Layla found herself back in her lounge room, but rather than being on the couch, where she had started, she found herself lying on her back on the floor in the middle of the room with her arms out. She blinked a couple of times and sat up. Layla looked to her left and saw that her bow remained in her hand. She stood to her feet, still suited up. As the armour and bow started to fade and an angel appeared in front of her.

"Hello Shar," said Layla with a smile.

"Hello, Layla. You and your friends have succeeded. The scene is ready for the crusade. Many shall be saved, and you shall bring a message that will lead many into the kingdom."

"I'm amazed, honoured and humbled that I could participate in such a way. But it's not me who will bring the message. It is my dad who is the evangelist. He's going to preach up a storm!" she said with conviction.

Shar stood and smiled.

36

CRUSADE

Asuitcase, wallet, passport, mobile phone and an open pack of
gum lay on the bed. The apartment, situated on the outskirts
of the airport complex, catered primarily for international stop-overs.
The mobile phone started to vibrate and ring its familiar tune.

"Hello, this is Kenny," he said raising the phone to his ear.

"Hi, Dad!"

"Hi, Layla, it's great to hear your voice," he said. "I was…"

"I'm looking forward to seeing you, it's been too long," Layla
interrupted.

"I'm really looking forward to seeing you too. I was just…"

Layla cut across again. She didn't know why she kept interrupting;
it was more subconscious than conscious. She was excited to be talking
to her dad again of course because it had been so long since they had
seen each other. But she had already sensed somehow that her dad was
going to say something that she didn't want to hear.

So she continued, "I thought I would call to say that you are
going to be great tonight! We have been preparing, and everything

is ready for you to come and speak and bring the anointing for salvation. I'm excited to see you and tell you about all that has been going on in the last week. I have had some pretty amazing spiritual experiences that you will be amazed to hear about. But anyway, we are all ready for you!"

There was a pause, "I don't know how to break this to you honey, but it looks like the flight is going to be delayed due to bad weather."

Layla's heart sank. She thought about all the preparation everyone had made for the night. 'All the advertising… you can't just cancel or even postpone something like this.' The opening night of the week-long crusade was sure to be a defining moment for thousands of people. 'He has to make it. One saving grace is that we haven't advertised who would be speaking. We could get a stand-in, but no one would be able to deliver like my dad.'

Being an event manager, Layla knew all too well that some things just can't be managed. The weather being one and flight delays being another!

"Oh, no!" is all she could say.

"You know what," said Kenny. "It's only the first night I will miss. I'll be there for the rest of the week. Layla, I have been praying, and I know that you have pastors and leaders who could stand in for the crusade, but I feel that you are the one to deliver the message tonight."

Layla's heart nearly jumped into her mouth.

"What? No way. I can't do that!" she blurted out.

"But you could do this. I've seen you speak before – you are great! All I'm doing is asking you to do is consider it. Pray Layla, ask God, see what he says."

Layla already knew what God had intended. Shar had said it

himself. She did not feel at all equipped to speak to an entire stadium full of people. 'Hey, maybe no one will come,' she thought to try and console herself. 'Layla,' came a peaceful yet firm voice calling her name. She knew that the crusade would be full of people and that it would be a success. 'Otherwise, our whole mission would have been pointless, and God doesn't 'do' pointless!' she told herself.

"I'll have to consider it, but this wasn't the plan. It should be Kenny Dorsa on the stage, bringing the anointing back home. After all these years."

"You are the next generation, Layla. It is time for a fresh move of God, for the baton to be handed over. Now is your time. It is your voice that the people need to hear. Just say what the Lord gives you to say. I'll be there within 24 hours. I'd better let you go. I'll be praying for you."

"And I'll be praying that the weather clears and you get here soon!" Layla replied.

As she put down the phone, she knew God was calling her to do this. She had been to the throne of the city. She had been a part of preparing the city to receive the message, and now God was calling her to be the one to deliver it. Being a guest evangelist was huge. She had only ever spoken to a few hundred people at a time, but this was the stadium. It almost brought her to tears thinking about it.

She breathed in deeply and let out a short, punchy breath, "God, if you are calling me to this, you will help me, and I will give it everything I've got!"

***

The stadium was full. Traffic was gridlocked outside. Many did not even know why they were there or what to expect. The car park was a flood of lights, and the sound of car horns punctuated the busy intersections. Some people just came out because everyone else in the city was. This first night was the moment that the team had waited for in anticipation. Tonight was the night that many churches and intercessors from all over the region had been lifting up in prayer. The main thing that made this crusade different from all the others was that no one knew who the guest speaker was. There were two reasons for this. The first being that the organisers had heard clearly from God that this was the strategy to adopt. The second being that the crusade wasn't about any one person, but about the message that God wanted to bring.

***

That night Layla stepped out onto the open-air stage. Lights blazed into her eyes.

The five sat together.

"Hey, where's Layla?" asked Caden.

"You mean that Layla?" said Tristan as he pointed towards the stage.

"She's the evangelist, and she didn't tell us?!"

"I guess she is, and no she didn't," Tristan responded.

They looked at each other and laughed.

Samantha said to them, "Actually, I got a text from her a few minutes ago. She said that her dad was supposed to speak, but his plane has been delayed. She is stepping in and has asked us to pray."

A hush came over the crowd.

Liberty looked out over the crowd and noticed people from her school including Principal Spurges. 'Wow Lord, I pray that you speak to him tonight. Reveal yourself to Principal Spurges!' she prayed.

"Friends, this is your appointed night. Right now is your appointed moment," she began.

"Tonight we all gather together to hear a message. A message that is perhaps the most important message you will ever hear in your whole life! It has to do with you, salvation, eternity and the way to everlasting life."

At this point, Layla thought that she might get some resistance, but there was none. The crowd was hushed, and people were expectant. It was a great start. With the Triaxial Identifiers in alignment, people were able to receive the message; their hearts were open and ready.

"Many of you may not even know why you are here tonight. You may have no idea what this message of salvation is all about. I don't know how you got here, who brought you, or whether you came alone. But whether you realised it or not, God has been drawing you towards himself. Some of you, he has been drawing for many years to have an encounter him."

A series of ripples went throughout the crowd of 50,000 people.

"That's right; you can have an encounter with God tonight that will change your life and change your eternity forever. The message of the kingdom of God is simple. We are all separated from God by our own sinfulness. Sin is doing what is wrong, and it is also failing to do what is right. At some point in our life, and if you are like me, at many points in our lives, we have sinned, and that sin earns us separation from God. If we do nothing about this condition of sinfulness, we will be separated from God forever. We will end up in a place where God is not, and that place is called hell."

Even saying the 'h' word, people were still listening. She felt the anointing flowing through her. Layla knew that the Lord was releasing people from bondage as they listened. Chains were snapping, grips loosened, and demonic claws pulled out, even as she spoke.

She continued to go with the anointing, "There is nothing we can do to save ourselves. In fact, much of what we do and think continues to condemn us every day. But the amazing thing is that God never sends a person to hell. It is our choices, our selfishness, and our pride that lead us there. Our choices are our responsibility alone.

"But there is good news. In fact, it is the best news that you will ever hear. Jesus Christ came to earth to die for our sins. He paid the price for us, a price that we could never pay. He was the one who came to die in our place to give us new life. All we have to do is to acknowledge our sin and our need for him. The way you do that is to tell him that you are sorry and then to accept him as Lord of your life.

"He has given us this precious gift called 'salvation' and also another precious gift called 'free-will.' We must exercise this second gift to be able to lay hold of the first.

"Let me ask you a few questions. Do you want to live forever? Would you like to live in heaven for eternity? A place where you find meaning, significance and fulfilment? A place where you have an intimate relationship with your creator? Would you want to receive this? Tonight I'm saying that you can."

"Go Layla!" said Liberty in a hushed voice to Samantha who was sitting beside her. Samantha grabbed Liberty's hand and squeezed it. The others all had smiles on their faces as Layla was declaring the truth of the eternal gospel.

"There was a time in my life when I was without hope. Depression gripped me, and I could find no escape, no matter what I tried to do to overcome it. I probably seemed fine on the outside to everyone around me, but inside I knew that my life was slipping away.

"I had heard the message of salvation many times before, but one night it was different. I went to a church meeting similar to this one and listened to the message again. I knew that what I was hearing was truth and that it had power. I felt the presence of God around me, not that I knew what that was at the time. It made me want to cry, though I didn't know why. My tears were releasing the pain of my past, and that night I gave my life to Jesus. He completely changed me. I found freedom. That night I had the best sleep ever and the next day felt like the brightest day that I had ever lived.

"Tonight I present this opportunity to you."

Layla gave a call for salvation, for those who wanted to accept Jesus as Lord. People started to move from their seats and flooded the altar at the front. From every part of the stadium, people came forward to accept Jesus, including Spurges! Hundreds of people moved forward, thousands of people came to give their lives to the Lord. As Layla looked around at those coming forward, she saw Angel-Light running through the crowd. She lifted her gaze and saw an ambient red light from the Elemental Stone colouring the sky mixing with a golden radiance emanating from the altar. Layla felt the surge of the Holy Spirit urging her on. Then, for the first time, above the stadium, through the glory-washed sky, she saw faces, many faces. The great cloud of witnesses, with expressions of joy and amazement, were intently focused on the souls coming forward. The witnesses were gazing at them like nothing else mattered or even existed in the universe. Each witness was following a particular person of interest to them, not just as spectators, but as participants in the journey of salvation for these precious souls.

'Thank you, Lord for showing me this,' Layla said with a smile.

She led the host in the 'Sinners Prayer.'

"Repeat after me. Lord Jesus, I come to you... I am sorry for the things I have done wrong... I ask you to forgive me for my sins... I want you to save me and to become the Lord of my life... Thank you for forgiving me... Thank you for accepting me into your family... I will live for you for the rest of my life... I declare I am now saved and I am now a Christian... In Jesus Name... Amen."

37

AFTERWARDS

Her friends jumped to their feet, over the moon with how well the meeting went.

"Come on let's go find her," said Trinity.

Trinity, Samantha, Tristan, Caden, and Liberty went off to find Layla.

Layla stepped off the stage shaking, with a huge smile on her face.

Linda gave her a hug, "Layla, you were amazing! You did an incredible job of delivering that message. We are going to run out of our new Christian resources on the first night. We will need to get some more of those 'A Fresh Start' books for new Christians."

On their way to finding Layla, Tristan bumped into his friend Shaun.

"Hey Shaun, how's it going?"

"Great man. Great preaching."

"Yeah, lots of people here too. Seems like almost the whole city."

"Hey Tristan, I've meant to catch up with you. Do you have a minute or two?"

"Of course."

"You know how when we went out climbing together the other day and we were talking about hearing God's voice?"

"Yeah."

"Well, I was thinking about what you were saying, and I asked God to speak to me that night. Anyway, I had this crazy dream."

"Go on."

"So I had this crazy dream. I was in the midst of this battle, and I was fighting demons, and then these angels picked me up and dropped me in front of a throne. Then I had to fight some more to get close to the throne. I woke up the next morning sweating. It felt pretty real. Then this phrase came into my mind, 'City Appointed.' After that, I thought of you and wanted to talk to you about it."

As Shaun spoke, Tristan's smile had broadened.

"This is what I reckon. Tonight, when you get home, ask God to speak to you again, then pray for a bit and see what happens. I think God is going to take you on a journey."

"I was thinking of spending some time with God tonight anyway."

"Cool. Hey, I better catch up with the others. Let me know how it goes. You free to do some climbing next weekend?"

"Yep, let's do it. I'll give you a call."

***

It was a blur for Layla once she stepped off the stage and many people congratulated her.

'Thank you, Lord,' she kept saying in her mind as thankfulness continued to overflow from her heart to God with each conversation she had. She knew that she was a part of a miraculous night and that

God had used her to transform many lives.

Just then the others found her. Layla was getting handshakes and hugs from various people.

Samantha ran up to her and gave her a hug. "You were sensational! So many people got saved!"

Caden said, "It was all worth it. Awesome being a part of this journey with you."

They all went home later that night, having talked with some of the new Christians who had made first-time decisions to follow the Lord, collecting the response forms and assigning them to various local churches in the area.

The week-long crusade saw thousands saved and was a huge turning point for the city.

***

A year later, the city's transformation was physically evident. Business was up twenty percent on the previous year – over twice the national average. Three churches in the city had produced albums. Caden's band had cut an album that featured on the national charts. A well-known film producer had also set up headquarters in the city, and there was the talk of a big budget movie to be produced using the infrastructure of Riverdale as a backdrop. Gallard High School felt like a completely different place to what it was a year before. The school was becoming respectable again, grades were lifting, and the Christian group became revitalised with fifty attending each week. Though Principal Spurges didn't go to the Christian group, he helped them wherever he could, with advertising and resources. The group was now outreaching and every week new-comers were attending.

***

On the eve that marked the first year of their collective vision, the six decided to get together to pray and thank God again for how he used them to advance his purposes for their city. As they prayed and came together more and more into unity, the vision of Grace Falls came into their spirits. They were standing on the top of Grace Falls looking out over the city. The city was aglow with twinkling lights. Darkness shrouded the landscape beyond Riverdale's limits. As they stood on the clifftop, another came and stood alongside them.

"Jack!" said Caden.

"Hi Team," he replied.

Then others joined them.

"Falcon!" said Liberty.

Seraph, Shar, and Trillion also appeared along with the angel with the four faces who had commissioned them. The six were now twelve.

'Keep that head in one place!' thought Samantha. The human face smiled at her as if reading her thoughts.

Together they looked out and surveyed the city as a gentle night breeze blew over their skin. The axes shone brightly. The city had remained in alignment and was growing from strength to strength.

"Are you ready?" said the commissioning angel.

"For what?" said Caden slowly, almost knowing what may come next.

"Your city is secure, but there are others," said the angel.

"Are we going on another adventure?" asked Samantha with a twinkle in her eye.

"Your fellowship was the first of its kind. Since then there have been others. But there is a city in desperate need, and we need your experience and faith on this mission. Do you accept the assignment to save another city that is appointed?"

The six looked at each other and couldn't help showing their excitement.

"I think we all seem up for the challenge," replied Tristan, "Where are we going?"

"You will see," said the angel.

The twelve remained for a moment, then faded out of earth realm.

A wind blew across the empty clifftop. Blades of grass quivered in the breeze. A puff of dust blew through the emptiness where the twelve had stood just moments before. Elsewhere in the world, a team was about to be deployed into battle, but here, on this night, all was quiet, all was peace.

EPILOGUE
- ABOUT CITIES -

Why do cities on earth exist? What is their purpose? Throughout history have people just chosen a location to gather together to build houses, buildings, libraries, parks, and churches? Or, has God divinely inspired people to create a place to gather in exact locations to bring his purposes on earth?

Ever since the very first city existed, the city of Enoch, there has always been a reason for every city that has ever been. They are reference points on the surface of the earth to mark spiritual regions and purposes across our planet. One city is not isolated from another. Angelic highways run between them, just as demonic pathways also form networks using them as reference points.

People who lead a city, or reside under the covering of one, must have some understanding of its purpose. It doesn't have to be a thorough understanding, but as a leader makes a wise decision based on knowledge and motivated by the welfare of the people, the result will be blessing and favour. The city as a whole will respond to good leadership and become great. A city's purpose may be to provide governance for a country. It may be to direct finance, education, social policy, scientific endeavour, or be a provider of agricultural resource or have an anointing for creativity. A city may be apostolic in nature, releasing national and international movements and leaders. It may have been established to provide religious and spiritual direction for a nation, displaying the power and presence of God. Every city has many layers to its purpose, but it will have a primary function and God places his people by design within cities to be a part of fulfilling that purpose.

For example, a part of the purpose of a coastal city may be to be a gateway for international trade. It may also be intended to release the word of God off-shore and to receive ministries on-shore. Over time purposes can change or be added to, for example, the addition of an airport opens the way for an inland city to become a gateway for the sharing of international resources.

If the Triaxial Identifiers are in alignment, it will function as God has designed it to operate. It will be a source of blessing and provision for the nation. But if the enemy has caused the city to fall out of alignment, its strengths and purposes will be used to advance the enemy's kingdom.

Every city is appointed by God to contribute to God's plan of salvation for humankind, but the enemy can cause a region or even a whole country to lose its way. The enemy will distort the atmosphere, take the throne, and remove the memory of its mission, plunging it into darkness. It is challenging to build a church in that kind of environment. In some countries, the only option is having underground churches. At worst, only a few individuals in the entire country have made Jesus Christ their Saviour, and they often live in danger of their lives. For these places, in particular, people around the world must join in faith and pray for believers living under persecution. Pray not only for their protection but also that they would be an effective witness where they live and that there would be an answer for the entire country to have access to the Gospel.

In the places where Christianity is more accepted, through prayer, understanding, teamwork, faith, and obedience, an amazing church will arise, and that church will be a part of the answer to the city and even the country finding itself again.

As believers in Jesus Christ, both as citizens of heaven and earth, we must pray that God's purposes will prevail. Pray for family and friends, believers and unbelievers, those in leadership and anyone who the Holy Spirit directs you to cover in prayer. God uses the prayers that you pray every day.

'The prayer of a righteous person is powerful and effective.' James 5:16B NIV

PURPOSE
- FOR WRITING THIS BOOK -

Having been a Christian leader in church for most of his life, Mike sees a great need for ongoing Christian discipleship and has a passion to provide this. This book opens up the world of the kingdom of God through the context of a Christian fantasy adventure novel, which encourages and inspires readers to engage their faith and to pray.

City Appointed addresses the fact that earth is the platform for a spiritual battle which requires Christians to take an active part. It gives insight into the spiritual forces at work across cities and nations and how we, as Christians, need to play our part in establishing God's kingdom on earth.

With insight into how to hear the voice of God and illustrating the benefit of working together in partnership with what God is doing, Mike seeks to encourage readers into living an active Christian lifestyle, which includes engaging in the spiritual battle that rages around us through prayer and steps of faith. He seeks to lift the reader out of being solely concerned for their own daily sphere of life, into having concern for the entire city, and even the entire nation, in which the reader lives.

ABOUT
- the author -

Mike lives in Wellington, New Zealand with his wife and three children. He is a communicator, an artist, and an author, who is passionate about leading people into freedom, and into encounters with the Holy Spirit.

He was a Graphic Designer for over 15 years, and now he travels New Zealand representing persecuted Christians who live in the most dangerous places on earth for the gospel. His aim through this role is to raise awareness and support for persecuted believers, and also to disciple the church of New Zealand into a courageous faith lifestyle.

Over many years Mike has ministered through the gift of prophecy in various settings, and teaches others how to operate in the gifts of the Spirit. He has written courses and books on the gifts of the Spirit, produced other discipleship materials, and written Christian fantasy/reality novels.

Mike's favourite verse from the Bible is 'I have set the Lord always before me. Because he is at my right hand, I will not be shaken.' Psalm 16:8.

RIVERDALE

B

ELEMENTAL
STONE
[CLIFFS]

TRIAXEL IDENTIFYER
[RED AXIS]

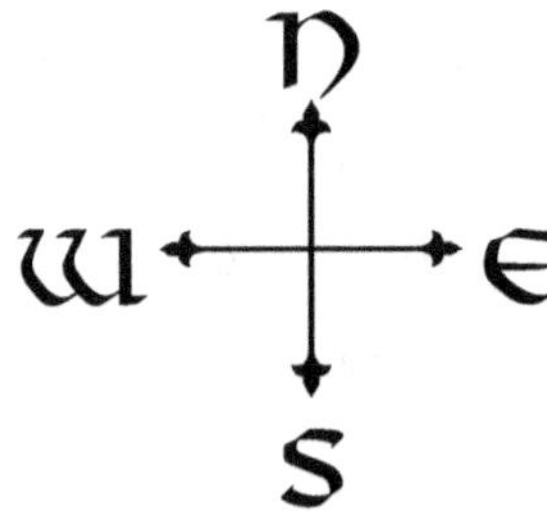

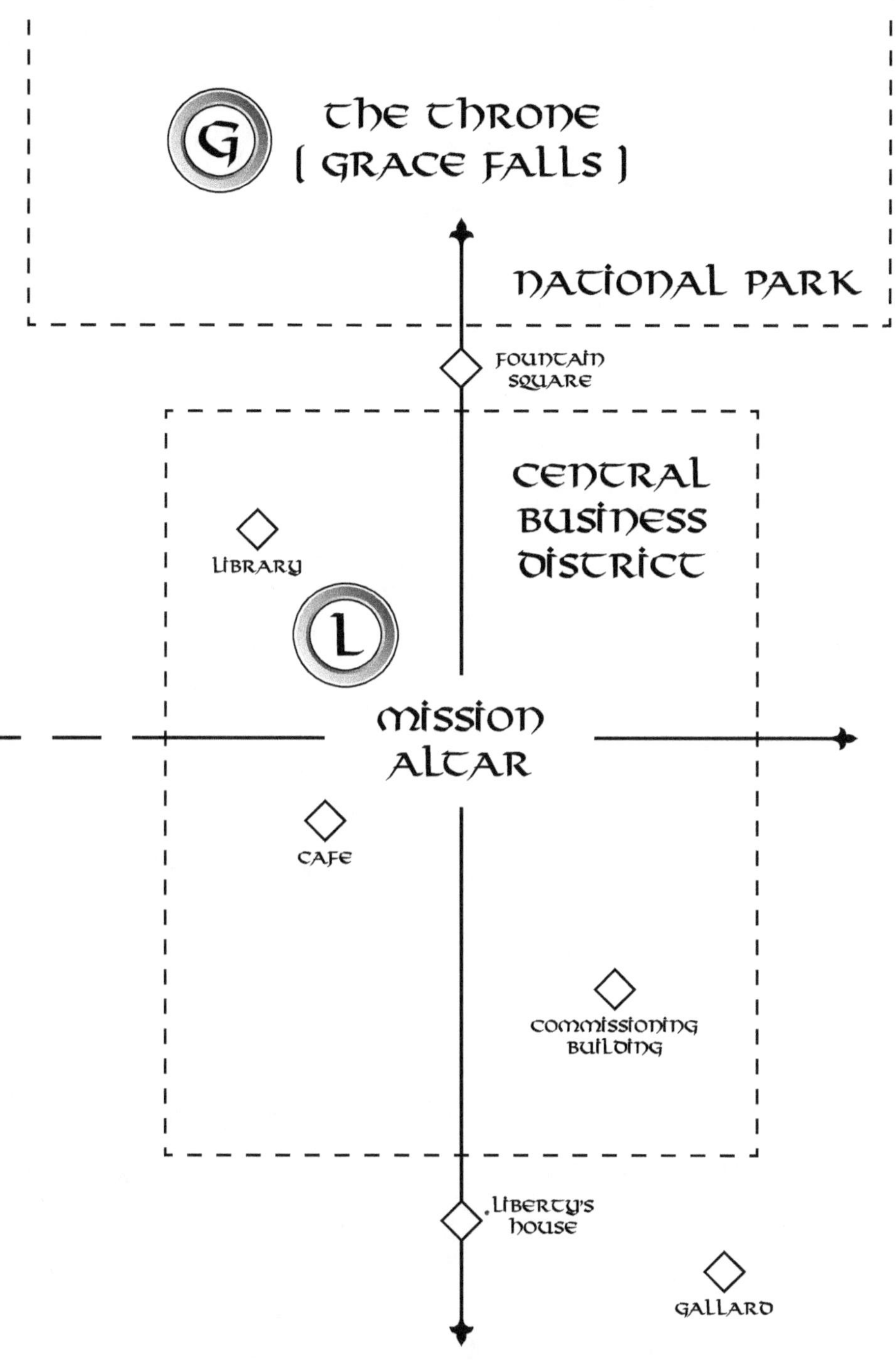

G
THE THRONE
[GRACE FALLS]
NATIONAL PARK
FOUNTAIN SQUARE
CENTRAL BUSINESS DISTRICT
LIBRARY
L
MISSION ALTAR
CAFE
COMMISSIONING BUILDING
LIBERTY'S HOUSE
GALLARD
TRIAXEL IDENTIFYER
[BLUE AXIS]

www.ingramcontent.com/pod-product-compliance
Lightning Source LLC
Chambersburg PA
CBHW050003070726

47592CB00018B/353